FUNFEAR

Judy Waite

Max clamped his hand to his mouth. He tried not to scream but there was a mad woman in the shadows. Her hair was crazed and wild. She was leaning oddly, waiting to grab him.

When Max moves to live with his dad, it feels great to be part of a family at last. But Max isn't the most popular boy in Dowton … in fact, if the local bullies have their way, he could end up nose down in a ditch somewhere no one will ever find him. But then he finds a way to escape. He can slip through his thoughts to a strange, dreamlike world that seems to offer all the fun of the fair. But the fairground isn't a bundle of laughs either. There is danger everywhere. And as the weird, magical world draws Max back again and again, the only thing that becomes clear is that Max has been called there for a reason. Max has to change time— but will time stand still long enough to let him do what he has to do?

Funfear is a novel that combines a story with creative writing tips and tricks, all twizzled together with the unique wordtamer internet writing experience.

First published in Great Britain by Wordtamer Press
Wordtamer Press first edition published 2011

Cover Design by Chris Townsend
Photograph Graeme Brimecombe

Set in Plantin by Alex Prior
Printed and bound in Great Britain by Lightning Source Milton Keynes

ISBN 978-0-956-9832-0-6

www.wordtamer.co.uk

WORDS OF WARNING

THE WORDS IN THIS BOOK HAVE
BEEN TAMED AND TRAINED BY

THE WORDTAMER

SOME WORDS MIGHT MAKE YOU SMILE.
SOME WORDS MIGHT MAKE YOU SCARED
OR SQUEAMISH OR SOPPY.
BUT WHATEVER YOU FIND YOURSELF
FEELING, BE CAREFUL,

BECAUSE SOME WORDS...

...BITE!

Tiptoe to the end of this book for wordtaming creative
writing tips and tricks, and visit:

www.wordtamer.co.uk

for extra wordtaming experience – learn to develop dynamic
characters, scenes and settings the 'wordtamer' way.

For

Jim Lambert
Headteacher
Locks Heath Junior School
1996 – 2011

With Thanks

ENTER IF
YOU DARE

I stared, almost hypnotised. A little girl stood between the trees that guarded the far end of the park. She was a long way off, but she seemed to be staring straight back at me. And there was something wrong. Something strange about her.

The late afternoon sunlight shimmered silver.

The girl seemed fuzzy. Fading in and out.

"That girl looks weird," I murmured. "Look. She keeps fading."

Sophie tucked straggles of blonde hair behind her ears, squinting round from the dodgy looking platform she was building with Jamil. "There's no one there, Max." She glanced sideways, nudging Jamil. "Max is the class clown. You'll get used to him."

Jamil studied me with his dark, calm eyes. I could tell he was trying to work out how someone as weedy and skinny as me could ever be funny. Or even interesting. Then he nodded in the direction I was pointing. "I can't see anyone either, but the human brain is said to contain roughly a hundred billion neurons. Perhaps, in your mind, you've invented an image that ..."

My voice went sulky as I cut across his geeky twitter. "Of course there's a girl there. You're not looking in the right place. She's got black hair. All long and curly like springs."

I wanted to tell Sophie to leave off telling Jamil things about me. I wasn't a clown. Clowns were stupid and boring. And sometimes, in dreams, they were scary. But I didn't say anything because I liked Sophie better than I liked anyone. She was the only one who hadn't made vomit noises about teaming up with me in PE earlier.

Well, Jamil hadn't either, but that was only because he was new to Dowton School. He'd soon get the hang of joining in with vomit noises and stuff like that.

The fading girl started moving. Drifting along the edges of the trees. Sometimes she bent to pick something from the long grass. "She's too young to be out on her own, I bet you she's from the Infants. She should be with a grown-up," I said. "And anyway, those woods are private. You're not s'posed to go in them."

I glanced at Sophie again. She'd gone back to laying planks of wood on carefully spaced bricks. Jamil propped a flat sheet of metal against the park bench and fussed around, making it level. They weren't taking any notice of me. I might as well have been invisible.

I made my voice all spooky and low, trying to make them look round again. "The ghosts of mad people live in those woods. The ones who escaped from that loony bin place.

I expect that's why they've banned everyone from going there."

"That's not it, Max," Sophie sighed. She turned to Jamil. "There used to be a mental hospital just behind the trees there, where Max is pointing. It was derelict for years. It's been pulled down now, but the land's being used for new houses. They've already built the first ones, over the other side." Sophie threw a quick glance back towards the fading girl, but she didn't seem bothered about her. Instead, she shuddered. "That hospital was a horrible place. It had towers, and windows like slitted eyes that seemed to watch you through the trees. More like a prison than a hospital."

Jamil glanced that way too, then nodded sadly, as if she was telling him the most tragic thing in the world. "Those old asylums were nightmare places. They used to tie patients to their beds, or lock them in padded cells." He didn't seem bothered about the girl either. Instead he pulled a flashy new iPhone from the back-pocket of his jeans. Just a chance for him to show off.

Neither he nor Sophie were in their school uniforms. Not like me. School had finished hours ago, but I hadn't made it home yet. Some days I couldn't stand the silence of our house.

I'd kept my jacket on so no passing teacher would see I'd pulled my tie off and bunched it in my pocket, but I didn't look good like Jamil, with his skinny jeans and sports-top. And everything and anything suited Sophie. Even leggings and baggy t-shirts.

Jamil held the iPhone towards me. "You could google that old asylum. Find out some key facts about it. It's awesome to learn the history of your local area."

I shook my head, thrusting my hands into my pockets so he couldn't force me to take it. "Who cares about the stupid history. It all happened forever ago." It bugged me that Jamil was so interested in everything. It bugged me that he had a brand new iPhone. And it bugged me that he was getting on so brilliantly with Sophie.

Jamil studied me for a moment, as if I was a rare sort of insect he'd never come across before. Then he put his iPhone away, turning back to look at the death-wish ramp he and Sophie had knocked together. "I think we've finished creating this masterpiece. It'll be awesome. A real buzz. Trust me – if you get the manoeuvres right, the adrenalin rush is incredible. Better than being on a roller coaster." He picked up his zazzle green skateboard and paced the tarmac path. Counting his steps, he grinned round at me and Sophie. "The ground slopes here, so we can tic-tac down and pick up maximum speeds before we jump."

I wasn't keen on daredevil dangers.

I wasn't keen on the way he was suddenly saying 'we'.

I pretended to be more interested than ever in the fading girl. I shaded my eyes, trying to see her more clearly. She was so small. Some of the grass stretched taller than she was. It rippled as she moved through it. And she rippled too. Everything rippling, strange and unreal.

From behind me, Jamil was rattling out pre-death instructions to Sophie. "It's best to keep the front of your feet near the bolts. And when you jump, you want to create the illusion that the board's actually super-glued to your trainers. They're not, of course – you're just rotating around multiple axes."

I didn't have a clue what he was going on about, with his stupid rotating axes. And I didn't care. There was a rattle and clatter as his wheels hit the metal sheet.

"That was amazing." Sophie had a bounce to her voice. All gushy and excited. I'd never heard her sound like that before. "We've got some real thugs round here, but I bet even they'd be impressed with you."

I hunched my shoulders. Trust Jamil to be someone who could impress thugs. My life would be a zillion times easier if I could do that too.

The fading girl was still wobbly and out of focus. It was hard to keep sight of her.

I heard a fresh rumble of wheels on tarmac. A bump and a clump.

"*In*credible, Jamil," Sophie breathed. "Where did you learn to jump like that? Did you see him, Max?"

I acted as if I hadn't heard. "I'm going across to check on that girl. I'm going to find out where her mum is."

I started walking towards the woods. I didn't want to hear about how Jamil had learnt to jump or tic-toc or super-spin through space. I wasn't too keen on meeting mad ghosts either, but it was still daylight. Warmish. The sky pale blue, with a few scuffs of pink where the sun was sinking. Mad ghosts would surely be a dark and stormy night time sort of thing?

"I'll prove to you the girl's real," I called. "I'm going to save her from all the lurking loonies."

There were more bumps and clumps. Neither of them answered. I bet they weren't even listening.

I shrugged. Who cared? Not me.

The girl was standing sideways on, just inside the edge of the woods. There must have been a wall there once, cutting off the loony bin from the rest of the park, but it had crumbled now. There were just a few posts and rolls of wire all grown over with ivy. The girl grew clearer as I went closer. She seemed to be sniffing something, but I couldn't work out what she was holding. Maybe it was nothing. Just sniffing air. I hoped she wouldn't scream and run when she saw me. She'd probably been warned not to talk to strangers.

Stranger Danger. I'd learnt about that when *I* was at Infants. Our teacher had said you should always be careful. Always be wary. I took my hands out of my pockets and wrinkled my face in a smiley, big brotherly way.

Shadows stretched to meet me.

The trees seemed to lean, pulling me closer with their snaggy branches. I tried not to think about mad ghosts. I tried to keep the whole smiley thing going.

I drew nearer and nearer.

A knotty, knobbly sort of tree loomed above me, blocking the early evening sunlight. I shivered. Someone had scratched a message into its trunk, and the words ran like a ragged scar across the bark.

ENTER IF YOU DARE

The girl turned to face me.

She wore a faded yellow dress, all patched and raggy. A shawl draped her thin shoulders, but her skin was soft gold. Like honey.

"Is your mum about?" I hoped my smile wasn't too much like a ghostly grin.

Her dark eyes stared past me.

Typical! Even she was hooked on watching the amazing Jumping Jamil. I kept the smile going, "Are you lost? I'll help you."

The girl seemed to shiver slightly. She pulled her shawl tighter.

And then she was hobbling out of the long grass towards me and it wasn't a little girl at all. It was a hunched up old woman. Barmy Barbara. Our scary next door neighbour. She peered at me with her strange milky eye, her voice all croaky and thin. "No. I'm not lost, dear. These trees are my friends."

I was so shocked, I froze. Couldn't speak.

Barbara's long grey hair straggled round her blotched, hideous face. She looked witchier than ever.

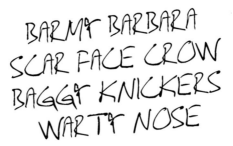

The school chant cackled in my head.

"I thought you were someone else," I mumbled at last.

"The light's always strange this time of day. I'm afraid it's playing tricks with your eyes." Her wonky mouth twisted into a nervous half smile, and her nut-brown face criss-crossed with wrinkles. She was carrying a wicker basket piled with pale yellow flowers. You weren't supposed to pick those flowers. There used to be signs up, but they all got trashed by those thuggy types who were going to be impressed with Jamil.

Barbara walked away, limping towards the gate.

A straggle of the stolen flowers slipped from her basket and scattered behind her, following her like a trail. I picked a few up, wondering what was so special about them.

They had a sweet, sticky, fruity smell. The smell was strong. So strong, I felt vomity and dizzy. I was about to chuck them away again, but then got scared some snooper might see me, and say it was me that had done the illegal picking. They'd be safer in my pocket. I could ditch them later.

I felt shocked. Stunned. And stupid. There was no lost girl. Just a trick of the light. A mad dance of sunlight between the trees. The dizzy feeling grew worse. As if I was the fading one. Perhaps Barmy Barbara had snagged me up in some wicked witchery? I didn't really believe all that witchy stuff, but still …she was weird. Scary. All those school chants must have come from *somewhere*.

I tried to steady myself against the knobbled trunk, but the ground seemed to be tilting. I closed my eyes, battling the sense that I was spinning. The whole park was spinning.

And it was then that I heard the voices. Strange voices. Ghostly voices. Sometimes close. Sometimes distant. They rustled round me like leaves.

Shadow-Thug

Max lay slumped with his back against the trunk of a tree. He could still hear snatches of the rustling voices, and strained to hear what they were saying. Were the mad ghosts warning him? Were they coming to get him?

His eyes were still shut, but it felt safer that way. He wasn't sure he was ready to come face to face with the spirit of a loony.

He tried to work out what had happened. He remembered Barmy Barbara looming up out of the woods, like something in a bad dream. Perhaps he'd bashed his head on a branch as he'd tried to escape? It made sense. He must have knocked himself out.

Above the rustle of voices was a sound like distant hammering; clatters of metal hitting metal. And just for a moment he caught the edge of something nearer. Something calling. Something shrieking.

Max made himself open his eyes. There were no ghosts leering madly at him. In fact there were no ghosts at all, so that was a relief. But something had changed. Even the air seemed different. As if a different blue evening had leaked into the springtime sky, making it dreamy. Magical. And eerie.

A sweet fruity scent laced the air, and Max thought he recognised the smell but he wasn't sure. Everything seemed uncertain. Like snatching at water. Reality was a liquid he couldn't keep hold of.

Suddenly a small girl slipped round the corner and into Max's view, talking quietly. "Poor thing, yer all shivery. I'll get Ma to make you a smart new jacket, when she's got a minute of time. I've picked some minty herbs for you, to help yer fur grow back."

Max's heart gave a jump and a jolt. It was the girl. The one Barmy Barbara had said was just a trick of the light. He shouldn't have believed her. She only had that one weird eye. She couldn't possibly see anything properly.

So there were definitely no ghosts. If the girl was real, then the voices must be real too.

He struggled to sit upright, and saw a muddle of trailers. Caravans. Tatty old trucks and vans.

"I just broughted you some scraps too." The girl wasn't talking to Max. She wasn't even looking at him. She was crouching by the nearest trailer, peering underneath and clicking her fingers.

Max stood up groggily, and peered too. There was something huddled there. A dog? Another child? He edged nearer, partly to get a better look, and partly to ask the girl what was going on.

The 'something' moved. The shrieking started up again, like strange, strangled yelps. Max jumped backwards, his gut lurching in panic. Whatever it was, it looked dark and hairy and dangerously scary. And then it loped out from the shadows and Max saw it properly. A baby chimp.

"Shhh, you old silly. It's only me, there's nuthin' to be frighted about." The girl clicked her fingers again and the chimp seemed to settle, snuffling and scratching its ear.

Max knew it was cruel to keep chimps as pets. Chimps like to be in tropical treetops, swinging about with their long arms. He learnt that from his teacher. Miss Kindly was always talking about wild animals and how they should be left to run free.

"Clover – come on."

Clover just kept on scratching her ear, making sad little chattering noises. Max was about to go nearer and see if he could help, when all at once the chimp loped forward and ran to the girl.

"Silly thing. You knows I won't let no one hurt you." The girl lifted the chimp, tucked the shawl round her and squatted on the ground, rocking gently. She began singing a soft tuneless song. The words drifted. Soft as petals. They filled Max with a squeezing sort of sadness.

The girl rested her head against the side of the trailer, and for a second her look seemed to laser Max's way. He waited for her to see him, but the strange, dusky light must have swallowed him. It was as if he was invisible. Her glance was nothing more than a graze.

Just beyond all the trailers he could make out posts and poles. The hammering made a constant clonk-clonk clonking. It definitely wasn't Sophie and Jamil. They must have gone off and left him. Max thought it was pretty mean of them, but it was their loss. They were missing all the action. Something new was being built in the park. Lots of things were being built.

"Don't eat me sleeve, Clover, Ma will get cross. She's only just stitched this dress together." The girl giggled. "Here – eat these scraps of tatty peel instead."

Max wondered how much time had passed? It felt like ages. His thoughts were still a bit muggy, but he forced himself to focus on home. He hoped Dad was working extra late selling windows, otherwise he'd be worried that Max wasn't back. He pulled his mobile from his jacket pocket, ready to text Dad. Let him know he was all right.

But there was no light from the mobile's screen.

No signal at all.

He wasn't surprised. It wasn't like Jamil's iPhone or anything. Just a cheapie car-boot sale thing. They never lasted long. Shoving the mobile back in his pocket, he half turned, squinting, trying to make out where the park gate was. His view was blocked by more trailers and vans.

"Bibi! Bibi! Where the heck are you?" A shout stabbed through the haze of Max's thoughts, followed by the sound of approaching footsteps.

The girl pushed Clover away, dragging the shawl back round her own shoulders. "Quick. Get yerself safe." The chimp scuttled back under the trailer again.

A boy appeared from between the trailers. Older than Max. Teenage. "Yer s'posed to be guardin' the wagon, Bibi. How dare you loaf around wastin' time here."

"I picked herbs for Clover, and brought her some scraps. I've only come for the littlest time. Sabre were asleep when I left."

"You stupid kid." The sound of the smack bit the air. It took Max a moment to grasp that the girl had been slapped. The chimp grasped it though. She let out a shrill screech, the sound jabbing like a siren. Or a warning. Max could see her under the trailer, all bristling and fierce.

"How d'you know there isn't a rabble of townies pokin' their noses round that wagon?" The boy lowered his voice and the whisper hissed like a snake. "You know I convinced the guv'nor my idea were a money spinner, and now he's pinnin' his hopes on it. The swap cost him his best horses and that baby elephant. If anythin' goes wrong, it'll be us lot he'll be swappin' next. In fact he won't be swappin' us, he'll just be chuckin' us out."

"Don't be cross, Danior. I were comin' straight back. But I knew Clover were all lonely and hungry. I didn't have no food for her earlier." Bibi had her hand up, covering one cheek. Max could see the blotched bruise darkening her skin.

"Feedin' that chimp is just a waste. It's sick. The punters don't want to cough up to see creatures in their death throes, and there's no room here for an animal that can't earn its keep, however soft the guv'nor seems. I've a mind to stick it in with the cat. It'd be over in seconds."

"No, Danior – please …I only feeds her waste scraps. She don't cost us any pennies."

"It costs us time."

"I won't do it again. I'll do all the things you say."

There were more footsteps.

Another boy. "The Top's up. We've just finished. I noticed you weren't out there helping, so I wondered if there was some sort of problem." This voice was calmer. Husky. Soft for a boy.

"It's none of yer business where I am, or what I'm doin'."

Max blinked, squinting again as he tried to take him in. The husky-voiced boy had a shaggy brown mane of hair that reached to his shoulders.

"Bibi? Are you all right?" Max noticed husky-voice had weird clothes on. Trousers with braces, and a baggy white shirt.

"I'm warnin' you to keep out of it, George." Danior's hair was very black. He had braces too, but no shirt. Max thought both of them would attract trouble from the thugs. They always had a go at anyone who looked different.

The two of them circled each other. Locking looks.

"Please, Georgie," Bibi's voice was trembling, "don't start brawlin' again." Her fingers plucked nervously at the fringed edges of her shawl. "Please."

George hesitated. "Are you sure you're all right, Bibi?"

And in that paused moment, Danior spat. A great ugly gob landed in George's mane of hair.

"You skunk." George sprang forward, his fist jabbing at Danior's jaw.

Bibi hid her face, peeping between her fingers. Behind her, still huddled under the trailer, Clover did the same.

Danior grabbed George's wrist, twisting it round. Max winced in silent sympathy. He knew a grip like that could burn. It could make you screech like a monkey.

George didn't screech. His whole body shook as he pushed back against Danior's hold. Sometimes one of them gained the edge. Sometimes the other. The movements were small. Their breaths were harsh and hard.

Max stood watching, wondering if he should shout or step forward and stop them. But getting caught up in someone else's fight was a bad idea. He'd spent big chunks of his life trying to duck away from punches and kicks, and thuggies who tried to wrench his head off just to pass the time. Wading into this private battle would be bound to end with him being the one with the black eye and bloodied nose.

So he just kept watching. Gripped with the helpless horror that always came with being too close to ugly scuffles.

Beyond, in the distance, there was still hammering. Max could make out threads of voices. Sometimes laughter. Sometimes sharpened words that would have made Miss Kindly's hair go grey. A heavy thud-thud-thudding seemed to roll out. Getting closer.

George and Danior stayed locked in their fierce but silent fight.

And then suddenly, from somewhere behind the trailers, something huge came looming. One small unblinking eye stared out through scabby grey folds of crinkled skin …

GALUMPHING GREY GIANT

… an elephant.

There was a real live plonking great elephant plodding straight towards where Max was standing.

Max's heart bucked. Panic froze him. He would be mown over. Trampled. Squashed into the ground like someone steam-rollered in a cartoon. The scream that might have saved him stuck in his throat. This was really, *really* going to hurt.

But the elephant stopped. Just in time.

It stood quietly and watched George and Danior, who both shifted away from it but kept on fighting. Not even glancing its way.

Max had never stood next to an elephant before. Never realised how massive they were. Its baggy skin was criss-crossed with wrinkles and folds. As if it was wearing a raincoat two sizes too big. Its trunk was wrinkly too, swaying with a sort of rhythm. A tired dance. It was wearing a red and gold headpiece, all strapped up round its head.

Bibi put her arms around its massive leg and it lowered itself gently, settling into an awkward kneeling position. Its trunk snaked round her, nuzzling her neck. "They won't stop fightin', Martha," Bibi murmured into its huge ear. "Is the guv'nor with …?"

Before she could finish, a red-coated man in long black boots rippled into view, waving a top hat and calling, "Come on, boys, a broken beak won't earn either of you coppers in the freak show. Time slips through our fingers like sand, and we've work to do before we bedazzle the uninitiated tomorrow." He strode closer, and Max could see he was very tall, with a cropped, bristly beard that seemed touched with silver. The red coat had gold trimmings that glowed from the cuffs and the collar. Bedazzle.

Max had never heard that word before, but he understood it. Bedazzle. It was a shining, sparkling sort of word. He whispered it softly, and it seemed to fizz on his tongue, like a bubbly sort of sweet.

"Stop now, boys. I command it. Before you pummel and pulverise each other into eternal darkness. What good could come of such ghastly grapplings?" The man marched right up to Danior, and tapped his shoulder with a white gloved hand.

Danior broke away from George at last.

The two of them stood glaring at each other. Max could see that, if the man turned and left, the whole fight would kick off again.

The tall man didn't scare Max, but he was odd. Almost

unreal. He moved his gloved hands wildly when he talked, like someone in a play. A pantomime. His words all learnt from some strange script that Max could barely understand.

"So now, you two, what boyish bickerings have brought you to this sad scenario?"

Bibi was the first to speak. "Sorry, Guv'nor. Danior come lookin' for me cos I left the wagon but I should of stayed where I were told. It were my fault." She scrambled away from the elephant and stood in front of him, hanging her head and staring miserably at the ground.

"Hmmph." The guv'nor reached forward and touched her hair briefly. Gently. "There's many secrets in a one sided star." His gaze shifted to Danior again. Danior held the look for a moment, then he stared at the ground too.

"We need you over at the Top, my trusted tamer. I'm planning new delights for tomorrow's show. Fresh line-up. Funtastic, fabulous acts and action. Got to keep all of you on your tippy-toes. And you, boy," the guv'nor jerked his head at George and raised one arm dramatically, "you must help where you can, and get the rides rocking. We need this park alive with lights. Everything whirling and wheeling."

"Yes, Guv'nor. Sorry, Guv'nor." Now it was George's turn to study the grass.

The guv'nor lowered his voice, as if he was sharing secrets, but the words still seemed to be carried across the night. Drifting away through the dreamy blue light. "I've just been out with my marvellous Martha here. As you know, the parade only drew a sorry few to line the streets, so the two of us went back round with candy sticks and toffee apples. Offering extra excitement. I want the good people of Dowton to come flocking to see what we have to offer. I want their pennies in our pockets, as just reward for all our magnificent motivations. And I'm sure you boys want that too." He smiled, his eyebrows raised.

Neither George nor Danior moved. Neither of them spoke.

The guv'nor nodded like someone answering their own question, and smiled again. "Come Martha, we've still got punters to persuade." He hooked one long leg over the elephant's back, settling himself upright as she rose to standing. "Farewell one and all." He winked at Bibi and tipped his hat, then rode away, both of them slowly soaked up by the gathering twilight.

The boys came alive again, as if a switch had been clicked back on.

Danior pushed George's chest, shoving him backwards. His eyes burnt like small fierce glitters of coal. His fists were clenched.

George stared back. A steadier look. But his fists were clenched too.

"You blasted josser. Now look what you've done. Got me the wrong sort of attention from the guv'nor. I can do without him watchin' me every move. There's things he's better off not knowin'," Danior snarled. "Yer bad news all round. We don't even know where you've come from. Who knows what curses you've brought with you. The guv'nor ought to send you packin'. You've no place travellin' with us."

"I do my job. He needs me."

"Don't rely on that." Danior spat again. "There might be a day comin' when he sees a different truth. Get movin', Bibi, you'd better get yerself back to that wagon. I'm goin' across to the Top, then I'll come and take over meself. I'm waitin' on meetin' an … er … business acquaintance there later anyway, so you can go as soon as I gets back."

Max watched them leave, Danior's knuckles on Bibi's back, as if he was pushing her forward.

George followed. And Max followed too. He felt drawn to them. Called by them, even though they didn't know he was there.

STABBING

The sky still glowed the magical, dream-tinted blue, but it was darker now. Like spilled ink. Drifts of pale clouds softened the darkness, and a soft splattering of evening stars shone like pinpricks in the sky.

All around, the park was full of skeletons. Skeletons of fairground rides. The bones of a Ferris wheel. A half-finished swing-boat frame. Posts and poles locked together, criss-crossed, all jutting and jumbled. Men and children were nailing up panels.

Max moved like a ghost between the posts and people, struggling to keep sight of the others in the darkening night.

The sweet fruity smell lingered everywhere, and from time to time Max caught snatches of music. A soft, distant funfair sound that seemed to creep through all the spaces. Eerie. Uneasy.

Up ahead, the others passed by a brightly painted stall. 'Clown Shoot'. Cardboard clowns' faces lay stacked on the counter, the top one's mad eyes staring up from beneath bright painted eyebrows. Behind them, strange glass jars lined the shelves at the back of the stall. They were filled with liquid. Things moved inside. Writhed and flashed and juddered.

Max hurried past, too scared to look closely. But his imagination swam with pictures of pickled brains. Floating eyes. Fat, sluggy fingers and hubbly bubbly stews made from body bits. He remembered that fainting feeling, and Barmy Barbara hobbling towards him. He remembered more of those witchy chants.

Barmy Barbara pickles worms
makes slug jam
and soup that squirms

Barmy Barbara eats
real fingers
she'll get yours
if you dare linger

Max wasn't lingering. He broke into a slow jog. He wasn't really stuck in a witchy spell. He couldn't believe that. But still, the park had gone weird, and it was full of strangers. Stranger Danger. Always be careful. Always be wary.

Up ahead, George stopped by a long-faced boy. Edging closer, Max stopped too. The new boy had hair like a loo brush. All sticking up and bristly. He was building another skeleton frame. Behind him, the track of a roller coaster jutted upwards, silhouettcd against the back-drop of the ink-blue sky.

"Keep goin'." Danior pushed Bibi on past George and Loo-brush. The evening curled round them. Devouring them.

Max hesitated, wondering whether he should keep trailing them, but then decided to stay near George. It was George who seemed most likely to tell him what was going on. And although George looked a bit older than him, he was still someone he'd like to know. Someone he'd choose as a friend – if choosing friends was something that could ever happen.

He hovered awkwardly, waiting.

The roller coaster train was parked up under a tree. The word *haunted* was dripped in silver across its black engine.

George grinned at Loo-brush. "Guv'nor's sent me out to cast an eye over what still needs doing. You want some help?"

"You'd save my life." Loo-brush nodded miserably. "I'm hopeless at putting these posts together and I don't work fast enough. Guv'nor's already picked me out as a lost cause. He took me to one side yesterday and gave me this gentle sort of chat about what it costs to feed us all in these 'troubled times'. How we have to earn every crumb. He can't afford to hang on to losers. I'll be out on my ear if I can't quicken up."

George picked up a pole and began fixing it to the one

Loo-brush was holding. "This is one of the toughest rides to build. Can't you wangle a job on something different?"

"There's nothing else going." Loo-brush's long chin jutted forward, his lips pouting as he shook his head. Then he shrugged. "But I'm working out an act for the ring. Got my sights on bright lights and fame and fortune."

George frowned as he fitted new poles. He worked fast. Fiercely. As if something Loo-brush had said had got through to him. "The guv'nor can give you more tips, once he's seen how good you are," he said at last. "He's done everything in his time. Started on the horses as a kid. Acrobatics. Tightrope. Ate fire and rode elephants. I reckon he's probably tamed and trained everyone, and everything. He's not just the ringmaster – he's the master of this whole set-up."

Loo-brush ran the back of his hand across his brow, and nodded slowly. "Even the way he uses words gets me giddy – the pictures he paints with the things he says. A proper word-tamer. You could get drunk just listening to him." Loo-brush stopped working and lifted a carved wooden chest from beneath a striped canvas. His voice dipped low. Sharing secrets. "I'm planning on wearing a clown costume when I do this for real. But Bibi's mum hasn't finished it yet, and I don't want to push her. She always seems a bit … well, unstable." There was a new edge to his voice. Half excited. Half scared.

George seemed to nudge himself free of his locked away mood and glanced up, still fixing poles. "She apparently lost her hubby during the war. Things must be hard for her."

"Things are getting hard for all of us." Loo-brush's tone sunk back into gloom.

"What d'you mean about wearing a clown costume anyway? Not being funny, but I can't quite see you with a spinning bow tie and a red nose."

"You're right about the bow tie. Wrong about the nose. I've nabbed one from Corky. But these are the beauties that'll make the guv'nor really tip his hat and take a decent look at me." Loo-brush opened the lid of the box and propped a wide silver knife along the edge. Then he pulled out a bigger one. And a bigger one. The handles gleamed, all studded with jewels. Max could see the blades glint and glitter.

George raised his eyebrows and whistled. "A knife throwing clown?"

"That's the plan. Fun and fear." Loo-brush was looking intensely at George, as if he was pleading with him to say something good.

"It'll go down well. The punters need new ideas. New angles. The guv'nor won't get them in through the gates with a stale old-fashioned show. He says that himself."

Loo-brush picked up the middle knife and polished the blade slowly with the bottom of his shirt. "My old man's a butcher. I was s'posed to take over once he retired, but I can't stand hacking up bodies. Blood spurting over me. The mess. The stink. It was a dead deer that really finished me off, though. I'd got used to pigs and cows and sheep, but someone had run the poor thing over and they brought it in to us. Dad insisted I should be the one to dissect it. For the practice." He shook his head, his bottom lip pouting again. "I kept looking at its eyes and they were magical. Like something from a children's story book. I just knew I couldn't slice into it. I told Dad I was going out the back for a jimmy riddle, but instead I kept walking to the bus stop, jumped on the next one that came by … and two towns later saw this fair packing up from out the upstairs window."

George nodded. "My parents tried to force me to do things I hated too. But …" he pointed towards the glitterbright blade, "… you still want to work with knives?"

"I've been handling these beauties since I was three. They're part of me. Can't give them up." Loo-brush raised the newly polished knife so it was level with his eyes. He squinted at it, then lowered it down to polish it again. He gave a strange, nervous laugh. "Only, I want to do something snazzy with them. Something clean and clever and smart."

George smiled and Max thought that, even though he and Loo-brush looked the same age, George seemed somehow older. Steadier. He wasn't sure he could really trust Loo-brush with his blood-chat and mood swings.

George seemed to trust him though, because he suddenly blurted, "I'd like a decent act too …" He stopped as sharply as he'd started, as if he'd said something he was already regretting. He worked in silence again, lifting the canvas and draping it over the poles.

Loo-brush stabbed a sign saying 'Ticket Booth' with the tip of the polished blade, then hooked it onto the front of George's canopy. He kept slicing the air with the knife. Shredding the night into invisible pieces.

Max decided this was a good moment to grab George's attention. He couldn't match Loo-brush's crazy knife passion, so he went for something more immediate instead. "I went on a roller coaster once. It was at Thorpe Park. Have you been there?"

George glanced round at Max.

Max grinned. George had noticed him at last! He kept on talking, "The ride was called 'Stealth'. I think you were really meant to be older than me to be allowed, but this girl from my foster home blagged us all on. It goes eighty miles an hour in one point eight seconds. I thought my head would get pulled off. Because of the G Force."

George's eyes widened.

Max's grin widened too. "I threw up at the end. I honked all over that girl. She wasn't very happy about it."

That girl hadn't been happy about lots of things to do with Max. She'd been in charge at the last foster home. She'd been in charge because she'd lived there the longest, and because she bullied everyone the most. "The girl gave me a black eye when we got back. I'm never going on one of those things again."

"Watch this." Loo-brush's wrist flicked as he spun the knife in the air. It shot upwards, then twizzled down, whirling like a firework. Loo-brush caught it by the handle.

George turned back to him and whistled. "Impressive."

Max started gabbling, determined to get George's attention again. "The foster home girl told me Stealth broke down once, and it took six hours to get mended. *Six hours of everyone hanging upside down!* She told me that once the ride started, when it was too late for me to get out."

Loo-brush picked up the other two knives. He juggled all three. Faster and faster. The blades were just blurs.

George nodded. "*Very* good."

"There's another roller coaster there too. A dead body spurts blood all over everyone as they zoom by..." Max's words trailed away.

Loo-brush had stopped juggling, and turned. His mouth still looked pouty and sad, but his eyes were blade sharp. He still held the three knives—and the biggest was aimed at Max's chest.

Max felt a different sort of sickness. This was a slower, more creeping feeling. Bile in his mouth. He'd gabbled on too much, and now Loo-brush wanted to kill him.

Max took two steps backwards, his own eyes trained on the knife. His heart shuddered. The blade was dazzling. Deadly. "Sorry. I didn't mean to ..."

Loo-brush's eyes glinted. He smiled an awkward grimace of a smile, showing yellowed tombstone teeth. And threw.

The knife curved past Max in a silver arc, almost jabbing his right ear. He ducked just in time. The blade stabbed a tree, lodging there. The bark split. Crumbling like dust.

Loo-brush threw again. Then again. Stab stab stab. The knives made a perfect circle in the trunk.

He'd missed Max on purpose, but the warning was clear.

"Time for me to go." Max kept backing away. "I was really just waiting for George. But ... er ... I can see you're both busy. Maybe I'll see you later, George?"

George squinted, and frowned. Max guessed he'd bugged him too.

But it wasn't safe to try and put things right. Taking two more backward steps, Max veered sideways. He walked away quickly, then broke into a run. All the time waiting to feel a blade slice his back.

HITMAN

Max slowed to a walk and moved amongst a new maze of trucks and trailers, wandering along the narrow gaps between them. Strange drifts of music floated out from somewhere across the park, but they seemed far away. Just dreams of sounds.

There was a trailer parked sideways on to all the others, and Max made out a tent pitched against the back end. Two figures hovered, stooped and shadowy, near the edge of its open flap. A lantern hung from a nearby tree, and soft light blurred along one edge of the canvas, just strong enough to help Max see where he was going.

Max didn't want to get a knife hurled his way again, but he needed to listen to the murmuring voice. He had to ask for directions to the gate.

Max slunk as close as he dared. He was touching distance from the first figure. He stretched one arm. "I wanted to check how …"

Then he jarred to a halt, his mouth locked open in panic.

It was Danior, his mutterings now clear enough for Max to

hear. "I need you to take his teeth out."

"You got the money?" Whoever was speaking made a gobby sound in his throat, as if he was spitting into the grass.

"I'll raise it. Trust me."

Max crouched low, shrinking back to the edge of the tent.

"When d'you want it done?"

"Pretty soon." Danior's laugh was a hiss of sound. Not a real laugh at all. "Our guv'nor's got us booked 'ere for a week. It's Monday now, and we go right through till Saturday. But I want it sorted sooner rather than later."

"Tomorrow suits me. What time?"

"It'll need to be when the show's on. I can slip away after the openin' parade. The guv'nor's just told me he don't want me on again till the final act. We need to get it done with no fuss. No one knowin'."

"Agreed. You don't want bad publicity. I've seen whole circuses sink from the weight of that. And I've got my own reputation to protect. I don't want bad publicity either."

"Then we're both wantin' the same things." Danior gave that hissing non-laugh sound again. "Soon as it's done I can set about workin' up my new act. The guv'nor don't have a whiff of what I'm up to, but once it leaks out he won't blame me. He's a fair bloke, and once he thinks it through he'll be on my side. I'm doin' this for all of us. Eliminatin' risks."

Max shook so hard he thought they'd hear his clothes rustle. Danior was hiring some sort of hitman. A hitman would be good at hitting. He would smash George's teeth out.

Max had to listen to more. He needed to know exactly when, and where. Once he'd heard all the details he could warn George. He would save George's teeth. George might even notice him properly. He might start to like him a bit.

Glancing round, the open tent-flap seemed like an invitation. A solution. The tent would be a perfect place for hiding, and listening.

The gap was just big enough for Max to slip in without touching the canvas.

Still crouching, he dodged through.

Max didn't think about danger.

He didn't think about who, or what, might be inside.

BLUE-FIRE EYES

Max clamped his hand to his mouth. He tried not to scream but there was a mad woman in the shadows. Her hair was crazed and wild. She was leaning oddly, waiting to grab him. Fear choked out of him in small hiccups of panic. He was sure Danior would hear, and then the hitman would take Max's teeth out too.

And then he realised it wasn't a mad woman. It was a mop with a rubber sheet draped round it. The mop leant against a wheelbarrow, next to an upside down broom. There was a rake there too, and a long forked stick.

Max stood, mingling with new shadows. He could make out an untidy stack of crates and barrels, all touched with light from the lantern glow. There was a pile of gold foil stars. More cardboard clowns' faces. A red-striped ball, split open, had dust grey stuffing leaking onto the grass.

Danior and the hitman were still outside, their words muffled and meaningless.

Danior laughed again and Max felt as if wasps had crawled down inside his jacket.

35

It was pointless being in the tent if he couldn't hear what they were saying, but it would be dangerous to creep back out again.

He wondered what time it was. Dad must have got home by now.

Max pictured Dad, red faced from running, searching the streets. How long before he called the police? It would be a bad thing if Dad called the police. The police would call Mr Snook.

Mr Snook had a file about Max and he liked writing things in it. He wrote things to do with what Max had for breakfast. He wrote about the mould on the wall of their house. He wrote down who he hung round with at school, even though Max made it up because he didn't want Dad to know he never hung round with anyone.

He scanned the shadowed corners of the tent, looking for some loose edge he could escape through.

And it was then that he saw the blue-fire eyes.

Very still.

Very strange.

Very scary.

DANCE OF DEATH

Max's mum used to tell him to count his blessings. A white lion gazed unblinkingly out into the muted darkness. Max counted his blessings. It was behind metal bars.

The lion was lying down, its body stretched across half the cage.

"Hiya," Max whispered.

He hadn't expected it to answer, but the fact that it didn't take any notice at all made him braver. He took two steps closer. Then another two. He was nearly at the bars.

The cage floor was coated with sawdust. Some of the sawdust stuck in the lion's mane. Bones of small animals lay scattered everywhere, all the meat gnawed from them. Max pictured the white lion tearing the flesh from the bodies, its teeth ripping through muscle.

A ramp dropped down beneath a barred door. Max hoped the door was locked. The whole thing looked rickety to him. That lion could easily butt the door open with its massive head.

Max suddenly wanted the lion to look at him. He wanted

a moment – just a second, when its eyes locked with his. He knew he should be careful. The bars might be weaker than they looked.

His blessings might be used up. Mum had never said how many you got.

But he wanted the thrill of the wild-beast look. It would be something to impress Sophie with. Maybe even the thugs would get to hear about it. A zillion times better than a stupid skateboard stunt.

Max lifted his hand and waved at the lion. The lion flicked its ears but it kept staring past Max, through the open tent flap.

He stuttered the air with his fingers, wiggling them like mouse tails, hoping wiggled mouse tail fingers might catch the lion's attention. They didn't.

Max noticed a wooden board leaning against the edge of the ramp. There was a half finished lion sketched on it, and some chalky writing that looked as if it would be painted in later.

AMAZING FEAT

Danior Darkus Dances with Death
in the Jaws of the Beast

Max frowned, puzzled by the bit about Danior's amazing feet. "Perhaps they're something to do with the dance of death?" he murmured.

And then understanding roared through him, so fierce he almost staggered backwards. It wasn't George's teeth Danior was going to get rid of. It was the lion's. He would make the hitman rip out its wild-beast teeth, and Danior's dance with death would be to put his head in the gummy pink cushion of its mouth.

SCREAM

Miss Kindly had adopted a lion from a place called Lion-Land. She said it was a place where lions went after they got rescued from circuses and zoos across all of Europe. She said a time would come when there were no performing wild animals anywhere in the world. Lion-Land was somewhere that was doing its best to put a stop to bad things like that.

She'd had this excited, glowing face when she showed the photo of her lion to everyone at school. Max had thought the lion looked bored. It probably had humans like Miss Kindly taking its picture all the time.

Now, remembering the moment, Max hitched on the idea that Miss Kindly would want Lion-Land to rescue the white lion. He'd tell her all about it tomorrow. He'd tell her about Danior and the hitman too.

The whole class could write a 'begging letter' to the newspaper. She would give Danior the bad publicity that would stop him from ever pulling out any lion's teeth again.

"Once I've got some help, I'm coming back. You can count your blessings that we've met," Max whispered to the lion. "As soon as Danior and his hitman have gone, I'm going to run for it. If I keep in a straight line I should hit the fence. Then I'll just follow it round. I'm bound to get to the gate in the end."

He felt buzzed up. Ready for action.

Straining his ears, he tried to work out if Danior and the hitman were still there.

There was nothing. Just a heavy, sleeping silence. He'd creep to the tent flap and double check. Then he'd get out, and away.

And then he heard something new.

A juddering, scratchy sort of sound.

One of the crates in the lantern-lit corner ... was moving.

Max tried to back away, but his legs seemed like liquid. As if he had no control.

The scratching grew frantic. Was it rats? Vampire bats? He'd forgotten how weird this night had become. Anything could be in there. Anything could happen to him. His heart felt squeezed. Dripping fear.

From inside its cage, the white lion stood and stretched and yawned. It had long teeth. Knife-sharp teeth. Its huge head dipped and swayed as it padded to the front of the cage. It butted the bars. They rattled. It stalked away to the back of the cage. Turned. Stalked forward again. Four paces one way. Four paces the other. Butting the bars. Ramming into them.

Max was trapped between the lion, the crate, and Danior. But it was too late to move. Too late to make any more choices.

The rat-bat crate seemed to shiver. To tremble.

And something was climbing out ...

THE CREATURE

Max saw the head first. Then paws gripped the top edge of the crate. A face appeared. The creature's eyes were squeezed shut with the effort of pulling itself upwards.

Outside Max's liquid leg panic, he noticed it had floppy ears. A patch of brown over one eye. And then it was out, tumbling onto the dank grass and landing with a bump.

It was a brown and white puppy.

Scrabbling to stand up, the puppy began snuffling along the edge of the crate.

Max crouched down, clicking his fingers in the same way Bibi had done with Clover. "Hello, little puppy," he said softly.

The puppy plonked itself down and scratched its ear with its back leg.

"Hey, puppy – Patches," Max called gently. "Come and talk to me."

The puppy scratched its ear again, stood up, and widdled.

It sniffed the widdle, wagged its stumpy brown tail as if it was pleased with itself, then pottered on towards the middle of the tent. Getting nearer to Max.

Max forgot about Danior and the hitman. Forgot about Dad. Forgot about everything. He loved the puppy's funny toddling walk. He clicked his fingers again, talking softly. "Hey, Patches - who owns you?"

Max had never had a dog. Never even had a hamster. Foster children weren't allowed pets. But now he was back with Dad, and they had a house, everything was different.

"Would anyone care if you weren't here?" Max could scoop the puppy up, tuck him under his jacket, and take him home. It would be the right thing to do. He couldn't leave him anywhere near violent thug types who hired hit men to yank out lions' teeth.

He could easily persuade Dad it was a good idea. If Max had a puppy to keep him company, Dad wouldn't feel so guilty about selling windows in the evenings.

"It wouldn't be stealing if I took you home." He suddenly wasn't talking softly any more. "If you escaped out through that tent flap, a fox might get you. Or you might end up squished on the main road." With every fresh thought, Max felt more certain he was making the best decision. "I'd be saving you."

Max edged right up to Patches. His hands closed round him, lifting him.

Except – they didn't close round him. Something was wrong. His fingers were numb and strange and he couldn't hold him. The puppy slipped away. Max was clutching thin air.

A rattling caught Max's confused attention. The lion butted the bars of the cage.

It was padding up and down again - four paces one way; four paces the other. Max stared at it. Horror seemed to flood his veins. Pumping through him. His gut twisted and knotted and his hands trembled. He made another useless grab at Patches.

Patches padded *through* Max and headed towards the cage. Max stared down at his body. His hands. His hopeless fingers. What had happened to him? It was as if he was here, but not here. He could see but not touch. Move but not feel. But this wasn't the moment to wonder, or worry.

Patches wagged his stumpy tail, and barked.

"Shhh." Max's warning was shaky. "This isn't a great time to try out your voice-box."

He made one final grab for Patches. His hands scraped the grass. He couldn't even feel the whisper of a touch.

Patches put his front paws on the ramp.

"No, no. That's not a great plan either." It was hard to talk. Max felt as if his jaw was melting. The words rolled out in strange blobs of sounds.

The lion stopped pacing.

He hunkered down near the back of the cage, facing out towards Patches.

"No," Max's voice was a squeak. A stupid, useless sound.

Patches scrabbled with his back legs, his paws sliding on the slippy metal.

He squirmed in easily between the metal bars.

The lion's eyes fixed on Patches' waggy tail, the same way a kitten's eyes will fix on wriggled wool.

It licked its lips.

Max battled towards the cage, struggling to stay focused. He had to do something. He had to stop Patches from becoming dead meat. Dead puppy meat. A sob rose in his throat, but he swallowed it back. There wasn't time. There wasn't time. He thought he heard someone calling his name, but he didn't turn to see who it was. He rammed himself through the bars. Felt nothing. Lurched forward and tried to grab Patches. Gripped nothing.

"Get away, Patches. You stupid puppy. Get out. Get out." Max made one last, hopeless lurch. Sat on Patches. Lay on him. Patches bounced through him, his tail wagging as he happily attacked one of the gnawed bones.

Max raised his voice to a terrified scream. "NO!"

The lion sprang.

PYJAMA DRAMA

"How are you feeling, Max, mate?" Dad sat on the edge of my bed. "I could get the doctor."

I sat up slowly. I was home and everything was normal. I noticed I was wearing my too-small for-me Spiderman pyjamas.

Blackness floated in round the edges of my wonky bedroom blind that Dad never quite got round to fixing. My car-boot telly in the corner was in shadows. It felt late. I couldn't remember getting ready for bed, or even coming home. My mind felt muggy and strange. Even the snatches of things I *could* remember seemed confused. "How come here? I'm what happened?" The words were muddled mumbles. I knew what I *wanted* to say, but it wouldn't come out right.

"The old girl from next door found you in the park a little while ago. You were shouting and crying. She brought you back. You weren't making a lot of sense but you remembered enough to tell her the key was under the brick by the front door."

I shuddered at the thought of being near Barbara. She

must have touched me. Her scar face must have been near to mine.

Dad was still talking. "I arrived just as you both got inside. I got you to your room and you fell asleep again. The old girl - Barbara, isn't it? - she thought your breathing was regular and you didn't seem feverish, so we wondered if you'd just fallen asleep out there." He ran his hand across his shiny bald head. "I'd sent you a message earlier. Asked if you wanted me to pick up a burger on the way back, but you didn't reply. So I got you one anyway. It's still in the kitchen." He reached forward and lifted my mobile up from my bedside table. "I took this from your jacket pocket and put it here in case you woke up, panicked, and wanted to ring me from your room."

He scrolled down to find the message he'd sent, holding it up for me to see.

Hi how u doing? Sorry bit late. U wnt burger?

My phone looked fine now. The battery must have somehow sorted itself out.

Memories muddled round me. "Sorry mobile was battery. Broken dead." I shook my head. "Little girl. Fair went up. Thug shadow smacked her face."

Dad frowned. "I think I should ring a doctor. You don't sound good."

"Don't. Not need dockie dockie doctor."

"Max – I really think …"

"The lion white was waiting." I felt my fist clench. "I'm scared he caught the huppy. Huppy buppy puppy."

"Yes, exactly." Dad's face was getting paler. His frown deeper. "Can you think what happened, Max? Can you remember anything?"

"Patches dadda. Maxie couldn't touch him."

"That's it! You do need a doctor. I'm going to go and ring for one."

"No, Dadda. Daddy …" I forced myself to make sense. There were reasons why I mustn't see a doctor. The doctor might send a letter to Mr Snook. Mr Snook would put the letter in his file, and come snooping round to check up on us. "No, Da-da-da-dad. I'm fine. Just not prop-prop-properly awake."

That last bit sounded almost normal. I hoped I'd get away with it.

And I did. Dad ruffled my hair. "Sorry, Max, mate. Didn't mean to rattle out twenty questions."

"Everything's OK." I plucked at the frayed edges of my blue duvet. My hands had fingers that could touch and feel and pick things up. I was counting my blessings. "You arrre right." I spoke very slowly, my mouth shaping the words. Pulling myself back to the real world. "Must I have fallen asleep in the park."

A fading white lion prowled somewhere deep inside my head.

A distant Patches barked and bounced and wagged his

silly tail.

"And you feel all right now?"

"Yep. Feel all right now."

Gold foil stars glittered faintly along the edges of my memory. Stabbing knives flicked an arch of silver. Danior and George and Bibi drifted like ghosts between the fairground rides, then melted to nothing.

Just a dream.

Dad glanced at his watch. "If you don't think you need a doctor then you should have something to eat, and go back to sleep. I'll bring that burger and Coke up for you. You can watch telly till you drop off again."

A white lion roared but the sound was like faraway thunder. A storm I'd never know. My tummy rumbled out a small thunderstorm of its own. "Yep – I'm fine, Dad. I feel good."

Dad drummed his fingers on his knee. "I'm not trying to push you and if you're really not well I'll stay at home tomorrow. Maybe I should do that anyway? I've got an early morning appointment, but I could cancel it. You know what Mr Snook's like. If he gets word that I'm sending you to school when you're sick …"

"I said I was fine." It came out as a snap. I didn't mean it to, but being ill would cause a new set of problems. If I missed school, Dad couldn't go to work. If he couldn't go to work, he wouldn't sell any windows. If he didn't sell any windows he couldn't pay our rent. Mr Snook would buzz in like a fly round dead meat.

"As long as you're sure. I'll go and zap that burger in the microwave for you. Knowing you, you must be starving." Dad fixed me with his fake-smile face. It was the face he used to persuade customers to buy windows they didn't want. He got up to leave, and then stopped again. "By the way, I cleared out your jacket pockets when I was looking for your phone. Found your school tie, so I've hung it in the bathroom to try and get the creases out … and these had slipped through a hole to the lining." He fished in his own pocket as he spoke. "Who on earth did you get them for?"

He pulled out a straggle of wilted yellow flowers and held them up. "You ought to know not to go tramping about round those woods. And these are a protected species. There was an article in that freebie paper. We'll end up with the law after us, which is the last thing we need. I'll bin them." He sniffed the petals, frowning. "Strong smell though." He sniffed again. "Strange. Sickly sweet. Reminds me of peaches."

PETALS OF BLOOD

"Breakfast is ready," Dad called from the bottom of the stairs. "Choco Krispies. Come down for them soon or the milk will make them soggy. "

"Thanks, Dad." I was struggling to wake up. I'd slept deeply. No dreams though. None that I could remember.

"Come *on*, Max." I could hear Dad puffing around. "I've got to go. I've got a day stuffed with appointments and the first one is right across town. Traffic's bound to be a nightmare."

"OK."

"I've put your dinner money in your jacket pocket. The side without a hole in."

"OK."

"Make sure you come straight home from school. No hanging about in the park. I'll try and get off early and we'll have burgers, and a film."

"Good. Great."

I heard the front door open, then shut. I heard Dad get in the window company's super posh car. The super posh engine purred into life.

I was still battling to wake up. I forced myself out of bed, my bare feet cold on the floorboards. Trudging downstairs, I went through into the kitchen. The Choco Krispies tasted disgusting. The milk had blobby white bits floating in it. Disgusting! I tipped the whole lot in the bin, and saw the wilted flowers straggled across last night's burger wrapper, wedged underneath a dead tea bag. I picked one back out. A splodge of tomato sauce had dried, blood like, across the yellow petals. I sniffed them, catching faint whiffs of the peachy smell. Trying to remember the dream. I got snatches of the funfair, but I couldn't get up pictures of anything else. Not properly.

The more I tried to think, the more the dream slipped back into some foggy part of my brain. Like my fingers grabbing at Patches' skinny body. Nothing to get hold of.

I wondered if I could revive the whole sorry bunch. Make the smell stronger. Mum used to slosh a few drops of lemonade into vases, because she said it made the petals open faster. We didn't have any vases – vases were a Mum type of thing, but I could use a jar or something.

Only then I started thinking about Mum, but the memories were more slippery than the dream. I couldn't even remember what her face had been like.

Scrunching the flower in sudden anger, I rolled it into a squidged ball. Yellow juice smeared out from the petals, staining the tips of my fingers. I grabbed a bit of kitchen towel and rubbed them clean. Miss Kindly would say I'd been smoking, or something! The whole flower was just a dead squidgy thing now. Even the smell was gone. I scrunched it up inside the kitchen towel then dropped it back in the bin.

What was I doing fussing with a poxy wild flower anyway?

Turning, I spotted the time on the cooker clock. 08.35.

I should have left ages ago. Miss Kindly gave lunchtime detentions to anyone who turned up late.

Lightning quick, I raced to the hall and grabbed my jacket. I knew I ought to have found some socks, but there was no time. Lunchtime detention meant extra maths or a spelling test. I stuffed on my trainers, knotting the laces. I'm rubbish at tying laces, but I can do a decent knot. I spun out of the house, stepping into the glitter bright spring morning.

The curtains on Barmy Barbara's front window were pulled tight, but I hurried past with my head down. She might be watching through a gap. What if she came out and tried to drag me inside. Put a spell on me? As I got past safely, I realised I'd never seen those curtains pulled open. Not in the whole six months that we'd lived next door.

I walked on quickly. The walk became a run, stomping past the stinky flats. Rude words and even ruder pictures had been sprayed across the walls. Beer cans and chip wrappers spilled onto the pavement. Our house was old and rickety, but at least it was better than the flats.

After the flats I took a left turn, heading past the crammed together houses on the estate, and making straight for the park. It would be a zillion times quicker than going the road way round.

I grew hot in my jacket. Dizzy. That weird floating feeling again. I knew the sensible thing would be to take the jacket off, but I couldn't remember how to do it. The air was peach sweet and sickly. Fuzzing up my thoughts.

"Faster! Faster!" A child's voice seemed to be calling out to me. There was music. Fairground music that got louder and louder. I seemed to be floating on the music. Rolling through it. My head started spinning. Everything was spinning. No. No. NO! I couldn't fall asleep now. I *had* to get to school. It seemed as if the whole world was going round …

THE INCREDIBLE SEE-THROUGH BOY

… and round. And round.

Max was staring at a roundabout horse.

The horse had magical yellow eyes. It plunged and rose, its golden hooves prancing. And another horse came, and then another one. The music throbbed and thudded and someone called out "Faster, faster," and another voice snarled, "Waste of time, yer doin' free rides for show people's kids. And anyway I needs her back by the wagon."

It was a voice Max recognised. Danior.

An ancient man stood in the middle of the roundabout, turning a giant handle and calling across to him. "Guv'nor says it's better to keep the rides going. More chance of the local punters hearing the music and coming to see what's going on. There's hardly any tickets sold for the show tonight."

Danior stood leaning on a spiked metal pole, scowling at the roundabout. The ancient man hobbled between the circling horses, and stepped off the roundabout onto the grass.

The horses rose and fell. Coloured lights were strung out above them, bright as lollipops. Sparkling. Bedazzling. Max saw Bibi and Clover glide by. Clover looked done up like a miniature circus ringmaster, dressed in a smart red jacket with gold trim and brass buttons. Bibi's mum must have slogged hard, making that overnight.

Bibi waved at Danior.

Danior didn't wave back. Instead he stabbed the grass with his pole and spat, "Ticket sales are gettin' to be a disaster. Punters prefer cinema or radio these days. It's the same everywhere we set up. An' it's gonna get worse. I've got a mate lives up in London an' he reckons he's had a sneak preview of these new beeby sea box things that are gonna change the future. He … er … borrowed one from some posh family he … er … dropped in on."

"I've heard about those boxes too." The ancient man took a tin of cigarettes from his pocket. "There's tough times up ahead. All the travelling families are going to be struggling soon. Fifty years from now and kids will hardly know what a Big Top is." He lit a cigarette. The flame from the match sparked a flash of light.

Bibi rode round again.

The smoke from the cigarette drifted in a lazy fog, then faded to nothing.

Max had the vague idea that he'd been wrong about this funfair being a dream. It was all real. And he had another vague idea that he still needed to get to school. Only school felt like it belonged in another world, and getting there suddenly didn't seem to matter.

Turning, he began walking.

He passed the Waltzers, the colourful cars gliding and rattling. Two girls hunched together in a red one, gripping the silver bar, while a man in a peaked cap spun them round and round. There was no one else on the ride. Up ahead, the '*haunted*' roller coaster hooted a ghostly warning that its switchback nightmare would begin. The front carriage rattled forward. Empty seats snaked behind.

A lanky lady strode past. Max got the weird idea that she was carrying a doll on a pink silk cushion, but she went by too quickly for Max to see properly.

He stared after her; she wasn't just tall – she was like a giant. A bean-pole giantess. And then his heart twisted with sudden panic. Someone was lurching awkwardly towards him, stumbling in star patterned shoes.

A clown. A scary nightmare clown. Loo-brush.

Loo-brush spun a knife up into the scented air. Max crossed his arms across his chest. "Hi," he croaked, his throat suddenly dry. "G-g-good costume. I like it." He nodded at Loo-brush's star patterned baggy trousers, held up with red braces.

Loo-brush just kept walking. Kept spinning his knife.

Max forced a fake grin. "You're great at juggling and stuff. Wish I could do that. I like the nose too. How d'you get it to stay on?" He knew he was gabbling. Knew he was bugging Loo-brush again. Knew he had a good chance of getting that knife between the eyes this time.

But Loo-brush ignored him. Instead, he pushed in front of the giantess, blocking her path and baring his tombstone teeth smile. "D'you have holes in your underwear?"

Max saw her pause, standing with her back to him. Her voice bristled with annoyance. "How rude, of course I don't."

Max didn't think it was a good idea to upset a giantess, but Loo-brush just spun his knife up in the air again. It twizzled upwards, circling over his head. He flipped round just in time to catch it, then whirled back to face her again. "Then how d'you get your feet through your knickers?"

She made the sort of tut-tutting noise that ladies make when they're cross, then sighed. "Not bad, I suppose. I expect the boys will like that one." She giggled in an odd way. A small voiced giggle. A doll sized laugh.

Max grinned too. He couldn't help himself. He always grinned when he heard jokes about knickers or bottoms or ladies' boobies. And he grinned too because Loo-brush wasn't about to decorate his face with that knife.

"It's my new act," he heard Loo-brush say in his flat, sad voice as he walked away with the giantess. "Knives are the only thing I'm any good with. I don't suppose the show's got enough of a punch yet to grab the guv'nor, but I'm working on it." He flicked his knife again. "What d'you call a donkey with three legs …?"

Max walked on.

A gold edged entrance seemed to glitter out from behind a gnarly old tree. The inside was hidden behind a red velvet curtain, but a sign propped outside read:

AMAZING MIRROR MAZE: 3D

Max liked things in 3D almost as much as he liked jokes about knickers or bottoms or ladies' boobies.

He dipped in through a gap at the edge of the curtains, hoping no one would have seen him slip inside and demand money from him. His mind was still dreamy, but he knew the cash in his pocket was for a school dinner. There'd be all sorts of fussings if Miss Kindly knew he'd blown it on a moment at the funfair.

Inside, there stretched rows of ornately framed mirrors. Some of them were curved. Some were rippled. All Max could see were mirrors reflecting mirrors, reflecting more mirrors. He stepped back. He stretched up. He put his fingers in the corners of his mouth and pulled his lips into a clown's-mouth face.

The mirrors rippled silver light and they didn't see him.

They couldn't catch him.

Max wondered if he needed special 3D glasses to make them work. Perhaps he'd need to pay after all.

And then suddenly there was somebody standing beside him. Not just one somebody. Twenty somebodies or fifty somebodies, or maybe a thousand somebodies. And they all looked the same. A boy with brown shaggy-mane hair. It was George.

"I thought so," said George. "I guessed it."

"Guessed what?"

"I wasn't certain at first." George gave a sharp laugh and shook his head. "This is amazing."

He started walking all round Max, looking him over. George's thousands of reflections looked with him. They shivered and shimmered. They went on for ever.

"I saw you yesterday, hanging about by the roller coaster. I thought you were just another josser looking for work. A runaway, like me. You seemed like a bit of an odd-ball, but then half the people here are peculiar in one way or another. There's Ben who's so bendy he can fold himself inside a bottle. There's Jasmine who can juggle upside down. There's Medina who dances on the back of a galloping horse. I thought you'd perfected an illusion. The Incredible See-Through Boy."

"I'm not a runaway. I live up the road," Max explained. "Smithson Street. Number 33."

George was still walking round Max, studying him from every angle. "And then later on yesterday you did such a special thing. An incredible thing." George's thousands of reflections mouthed what he was saying.

"What did I do? What was the incredible thing?"

"You yelled when the puppy got in with Sabre, our new

white cat," George said. "I'd been heading over to the wagon because it's my job to do a final check on the locks at night. I heard you shout, so I rushed in like someone with a grenade stuffed down their trousers. I thought maybe some drunken local had got in the cage. Someone real."

"I am someone real." Max stared into one of the mirrors. George stared back out. Max tried to get his head round the thought he'd actually saved Patches. His shouting had warned George. He'd done an incredible thing.

"What happened to the puppy? To Patches?"

George's grin widened. "You even gave him a name? We haven't done that yet. Bibi's mum only found him yesterday, when she went searching for scraps of material she could use for the costumes. He was tied up in a sack, then dumped round the back of the madhouse. I don't reckon he'd have survived the night."

"Who would've done a thing like that?"

"Impossible to say." George shrugged. "We find lots of abandoned animals when we pitch up near woods, or on scrub-land. We often get the blame for it. But most travelling folk are decent to their animals. Animals are their bread and butter." His face tensed up suddenly. "Of course, there's always the exception."

"Is Patches OK?" Max remembered that George hadn't finished telling him the ending. "You got him out of the cage?"

"Sabre listens to me. I got there in time, all thanks to your yelling. And now Bibi's begging to keep the puppy. I expect her mum will let her. She lives in her own world these days. What with that, and being overworked repairing costumes, she probably won't even notice." George frowned at Max. "Can you come and go whenever you want? Have you got any control?"

"Dad wants me home early tonight. I wasn't well yesterday, so I mustn't push my luck."

"The illness is probably your last memory." George turned away from the mirrors and faced Max square on. "Have you been here a long time?"

Max scrunched his face up, trying to remember. Time seemed strangely meaningless. He forced his mind back to the moment when he'd found himself by the roundabout. "Probably about ten minutes," he said at last.

George laughed, but his eyes were kind. "More like ten months, I expect. But then your clothes are odd too, so maybe it's even ten years."

Max wondered if George was being rude about his jacket? Maybe it was obvious it was only second-hand?

"What was your name?" George said gently.

"Max Baxter. It's still my name now."

George grinned again, and raised one eyebrow. Max was impressed by the one eyebrow. He'd never been able to do that.

George raised his right hand and held his palm open to Max. "Can I touch you?"

Max lifted his own hand because he didn't know what else to do. He wondered if it might be going to be some sort of trick. The girl in the foster home had played tricks like that sometimes. She pretended to touch him, and then ran off and poked someone else, saying 'Baxter bugs, pass them on.'

George's fingers tilted.

A thousand Georges tilted their fingers towards nothing, and nobody.

Max tilted his fingers back towards George.

He could see George's hand tremble, as if he was straining for something. Waiting for something. George's eyes were green. There were gold flecks in the centres, like a scattering of glitter. Max felt weird being stared at for so long. He wanted to look away, but thought George might think he was rude.

He could feel his ears flushing up pink. They always did that when he got embarrassed.

Then George jumped backwards.

A thousand reflections jumped with him.

The mirrors seemed to shiver with the rush.

"Amazing! But bizarre." George made a fist of his hand and rubbed it against his jacket. "You've made me go goose-pimply."

"Why?"

"You honestly don't know?"

"Know what?"

"It's because you're dead," George said quietly. "No one on earth can ever touch you again."

RUNAWAY

"You're playing a trick on me." Max still felt fuzzy. His mind soft as candyfloss.

George's eyes were sad. "I'm sorry," he said softly. "I thought you'd have known."

The mirrors sparkled. Max walked up to the nearest one. It was curved. He lifted his hand again, pressing it with his palm. Pressing thin air.

"Do you have any idea what you did before you came here?" George watched Max carefully. "What was the last thing you remember?"

"I was stood by the roundabout. Bibi was riding one of the horses."

"No. Before that."

"I was late for school. Running."

"Did you fall? Did you bang your head?"

Max didn't answer, but he thought George was taking the trick too far.

The foster home girl used to take tricks too far. That was what Mr Snook said when he moved Max to a different foster home. He said the girl wasn't a bad person but no one had given her any rules in life, and she just didn't know when to stop.

The girl hadn't known when to stop about wrapping Max in brown sticky tape and dumping him in the wheelie bin. She'd stuck the lid down too. The bin wasn't full, but it stank.

"I'm sorry." George's voice was soft. "It can't be an easy thing to hear."

And suddenly a storm seemed to break in Max. He felt a thundering anger. He was furious with George and the foster home girl. Furious with anyone who'd ever played tricks on him. He tried to kick the mirrored glass. Tried to bash it. He spun round and pummelled George in the chest. His fists punched right through him. "Stop this stupid trick now. Please."

He had said 'please' to the foster home girl.

She had laughed.

It's not always a good idea to say 'please' to someone who is tricking you.

At least George wasn't laughing.

Max stopped the pummelling and sank down onto his knees. His fists stayed clenched. He stared at the grass, his eyes swimming with tears he didn't want George to see. A dribble of snot dripped off the end of his nose and he wiped it away with the back of his hand.

"I'll help you if I can." George hadn't flinched. Not even when Max was pummelling him. "There must be a record of you somewhere. I could check at the local graveyard, after I've cleaned the cages."

Max looked up at him. He got back to his feet. "I'm coming with you." His voice was shaky, and his head was muddled. He didn't know what to think. Or feel. "I don't think you're right about me being dead. Not unless you can really find a grave with my name on it."

George's gaze was steady. Sad. "It must be a dreadful shock. I'm sorry to have been the one to tell you. But maybe hunting down your grave will be just the thing to help you – it might set you free. Knowing the truth. But I've got to tidy the girls first, and then Sabre. After that I should have half an hour. Is the church far away?"

Max shrugged. He didn't actually have a clue where it was, but he liked the idea of hunting for it with George. He liked the idea of spending any sort of time with George. George had called him 'incredible'. It was almost worth being dead, just to have someone say that. "We'll find it. Who are the girls?"

"The other big cats. Three of them. They're the main part of Danior's act – at the moment."

Max thought he should tell George about the hitman, but then he might go storming off to fight Danior again, and he didn't want him to go away. Not yet. Not when George was just starting to like him.

They walked outside, and Max noticed for the first time that he couldn't touch the door frame. There was a softness beneath his trainers. The ground rolled slightly, like walking on water.

The strange fairground music floated round them. The waltzer whirled. The roller coaster hooted and the train edged up its switchback track. The peach scent drifted and a scrunched up flower floated across Max's mind. Was this a dream? Where did the dream start, and where did it stop?

The lanky giantess appeared again, still carrying the doll on its pink silk cushion. Max had a proper view of it this time. It wore a white dress, all puffed up, like a fat soft mushroom. The mushroom dress hid the doll's legs and feet.

"Why is she carrying that doll?" Max whispered.

"It's not a doll." George led Max round the side of a trailer, to where a tattooed man was brushing Martha with a broom. He whistled as he worked, and Martha's trunk swayed from side to side, as if she was trying to keep up with the tune.

George patted Martha, grinned at the man, and walked on.

"It might look like a doll, but it's actually a living, breathing woman called Little Lily. She was born without legs. Just a torso. Stella the Stilt Walker looks after her. They share an act together. A lot of folk like Lily end up as travelling show people."

"Why?" They passed the roundabout.

The ancient man turned the handle.

The horses rose and fell.

Max couldn't see Bibi or Danior any more.

"Punters pay to see them. If folk can't earn money, they often get locked up in madhouses. No one knows what else to do with them."

Max wondered if he should ask what a torso was, but he didn't want George to think he was stupid. "The madhouse that was near here is gone now. They've built new houses. But some people say the ghosts of the loonies still haunt the woods."

"I wish it *had* gone." George shook his head and pulled a face. "Madhouses are wicked places. Lily tells me stories about them. Nurses can be horribly cruel."

"My mum was in hospital. The nurses were kind in there."

"Has your mum died yet, too? Do you know?"

Max didn't answer. Some things were too hard to say out loud.

They turned another corner, passing a trailer with the words 'Danior Darkus: Lion Tamer' painted along the side. A brown bear was tied to the bumper. George patted its mangy fur. "Good girl, Natty. I'll come and chat to you later."

The bear shifted slightly, snuffling. It had a muzzle on its nose, and its eyes were weeping slightly, as if it was crying. "Poor Natty," George murmured. "I'll give you a clean up too, once I've come back from hunting down Max's bones."

Max got a sudden picture of how his bones might look. They were yellowy white, laid out neat and straight. As if he'd died lying flat on his back, staring up at the sky. He wasn't sure it would be particularly comfortable, staying so tidy for ever and ever. And then he thought that it didn't matter because George was wrong and he wasn't dead. Just dreaming. Max had to keep making himself remember he was only dreaming.

Soft footsteps came bouncing up behind them. "Who's that Max you was just tellin' Natty about?"

Max looked round, and there was Bibi, clutching Patches. He felt a swell of happiness, seeing the puppy's head poking out from Bibi's shawl. HE – Max Baxter – had saved him from the lion's jaws. And he wished he could stretch forward and stroke those soft brown ears. He wished he could take him from Bibi and hug his patchy body. But he knew better than to even try. His dreamworld fingers wouldn't be able to touch Patches. Not now, and not ever.

Bibi slipped her free hand into George's, skipping to keep up. Patches' head bobbed about, and his ears flipped and flopped with the movement. "Who's Max, Georgie?" Bibi repeated.

George glanced at Max, grinned, and did the one eyebrow thing again. "He's a friend. From a long time ago."

"From before you runned away?" Bibi's curls danced as she skipped.

"I suppose you *could* say that." George kept looking at Max, and grinning.

Max made himself grin back. It was a slow grin. An uncertain grin. And then suddenly he stretched his mouth into a wide, proper smile. George had just called him a friend. An actual friend. He couldn't remember anyone ever saying that to him before.

"Will you tell me the runnin' away story? Did your ma and da chase after you to get you back?"

Max stopped grinning about being George's friend, and

made himself listen. Some of the kids in his foster homes had run away. Max never had, although he'd thought about it a lot.

"They didn't chase me. I think they were glad to see the back of me. It was too hard to fit in with my parents when I was sent home from the farm. I spent two more years away, after the war ended, but then my father decided a life in the country wasn't what he'd had mapped out for me. He ordered me home, because he wanted me to go to a posh school and take tiresome exams. But I'd got a taste for the outdoor life. And for working with animals."

"I wish my da would be sent home. I never even knowed him, but Ma says he were extra special," said Bibi. "Does God ever send special persons back from Heaven?"

George put his arm round her shoulder and she dipped her head against his waist. "It's the special persons God wants with him most of all," he said.

Max felt a thick, choking sadness. The sadness wrapped round him and he couldn't walk. Couldn't move. Couldn't see. There was a timeless, endless moment when he tried to talk, tried to call out. But no words would come.

He made a grab at George but his fingers clutched air. He snatched for him again. George grew fainter. Him and Bibi and Patches all slipping away.

"You're going again, aren't you? You can't control it after all." George's voice was fainter too. "I'll find that grave for you, my friend. I'll keep looking till I get some answers."

BULLIED

Someone poked me in the back. "Hey, Max, I like your outfit."

My trembling turned into a jolt of panic; Danior was after me with that pole.

I turned and saw that it wasn't Danior. It was two of my worst nightmare people. Gabby Dobbs from school. And Scuffer, her thuggy brother.

And I was out in the street, round the other side of the park and outside the chip shop. The shop was closed but a bag of chips lay squished on the pavement. Flies muzzed round it.

The air was warm but it didn't smell of peaches. Or even chips. I stared up at the sky. There were no clouds. The day was glittery bright and the sky stretched an endless blue.

Gabby and Scuffer jostled me with their elbows. I stumbled forward. Scuffer hustled really close, waving a rusty tent peg at me. "You're a real fashion icon, aren't you?"

Gabby giggled. "Love that smart gear you've come out in! Maybe you should do some modelling? You've got the bum for it, after all."

I struggled to answer but my brain was slurred. "How here am I?" I managed.

"I think you're still asleep." Gabby moved in front of me.

Scuffer came up level with Gabby. His laces were undone on his trainers. I hoped he'd fall over. Miss Kindly gets cross when anyone at school has their laces undone. She says they are 'an accident waiting to happen'.

Scuffer thrust his face close to mine. He had a stubbly chin, the stubble mixed up with scratches and spots. I forced my brain to think in a sensible way. I forced my mouth to say sensible words. "I need to get to school." My voice was thick and slow but at least my words were in the right order. "I going to be late."

Gabby and Scuffer made copycat voices.

He going to be late.

He going to be late.

"Bunk off like Gabby. We'll teach you some lessons. More than you'll ever learn at that dump." Scuffer's voice was sneery. I already knew about the sorts of lessons he and Gabby would teach me. Miss Kindly, and detention, suddenly didn't seem so bad.

They hustled me on towards the main road, both of them behind me again. Every now and then they poked me in the back.

How had I fallen asleep in the park again?

Was I going loopy?

Perhaps I really was ill?

A white van honked and swerved, jolting me back into the moment. The van missed hitting a ginger cat by millimetres. The cat veered sideways, its tail stuck up like a fluffy pole as it raced away into the nearest garden.

"Shame it got away," said Scuffer. "Would have been a laugh to see all its intestines oozing out. Don't you think, Max?"

"Max doesn't think," giggled Gabby. "He's got a brain the size of a baked bean."

I felt that poke in my back again, and wondered if I could get away once we reached the precinct. I could dive into Sophie's mum's hairdressing salon. Beg her for help. But even as I thought it, I knew it would be useless. I couldn't tell Sophie's mum. I couldn't tell anyone. What could they do, except call the police? The school? The news that I wasn't 'coping' would be bound to find its way to Mr Snook.

"Just keep going." There was a change in Scuffer's voice. A steel sharp edge to it. I heard a ripping noise and felt something sharp on my back. It slid down the length of my spine. "Sorry about your jacket," Scuffer laughed.

I realised he'd ripped the seam open with the rusty tent peg. I kept going. And kept going. There was nothing else I could do.

We reached a petrol station. Cars thrummed in and out.

"Don't you dare try anything," Scuffer warned again. "And don't stop. Not even at the Entrance or Exit."

I didn't stop. I just kept walking, even though a black car had to brake and the driver made an angry fist shape with his hand.

A woman tottered towards us. Her blood-red high heels stabbed the pavement.

And suddenly I didn't care about Mr Snook knowing. I was going to beg the tottering woman for help. I took a deep breath. "Please ..."

And then a dented silver car clonked up beside us, hooted, and skidded to a halt. The driver was Karl Blade. Karl Blade had been to prison. Karl Blade was a zillion times more dangerous than Scuffer or Gabby.

Karl Blade wound the window down and leant across the passenger seat towards Scuffer. Music boomed out, and he had to shout. "Wanna lift?"

"Sounds good," Scuffer yelled back. I glanced sideways at him. He was grinning stupidly, as if Karl Blade had told him a joke.

The dented silver car was a bad thing for me. It was something they could bundle me into, drive me to a deserted warehouse, and tie me in a sack. They could leave me trapped there until the rats ate me.

Scuffer opened the front passenger door. He seemed to have forgotten about me.

"I'm coming too." Gabby gave me one last shove in the side. "Get lost, Bean-brain. Sorry we can't keep you company any longer, but we've just had a better offer." She snatched at the handle of the back door and scrambled in.

The boom-boom music was paused for a moment.

Scuffer settled in the front. "My sister's a pain," I heard

him say. "We can be rid of her pretty quick though. Just drop her at her dump of a school."

"You pig, Scuffer! That's not fair. And you know I can't go to school now. It was you that phoned in sick for me, pretending to be Dad."

"Tell them you got better. A miraculous recovery." Scuffer laughed. "Once we've dumped my annoying little sissy we can go back to my place, if you like. There's no one in, so we can do whatever we like."

"Thanks for the invite. I could do with somewhere to hole up for a couple of hours." Karl Blade laughed too.

They were both laughing like mad hyenas.

The boom-boom music started up again. The car window closed.

Gabby sat slumped in the back seat, her face like thunder. She stuck her tongue out at the back of Scuffer's head, and then turned for one last look at me, as if somehow it was all my fault.

A filthy black cloud belched out of the exhaust as they rattled away. I was left standing on the pavement, and the relief that they were gone made my knees weak. But there was no way I was going to school now. Not with Gabby around. And anyway, I was so stupidly late, I'd end up in detention for a week. I'd have to bunk off after all. I'd go home, but I wouldn't ring Dad. I'd just wait for him to finish work, and then tell him I'd felt too ill after all. He'd make a bit of a fuss, but at least he wouldn't have missed any window selling appointments.

I couldn't head home the way I'd come. Once Karl Blade

and Scuffer had dropped Gabby off, they'd be driving back in that direction, and they might decide they hadn't actually finished with me yet. I still had the warehouse rats in my mind.

There was only one other way, and that was to get in through the back of the woods.

I'd have to risk the ghosts of those mad people.

BUNKING OFF

I raced through the shopping precinct, dodging mums and grannies and babies in buggies. I passed 'Watch-it' DVD hire. It was all boarded up with a sign saying:

TO LET

Someone had painted an 'i' in the middle of the two words, which made it say 'toilet'. It would have been funny – on a different sort of day. Sophie's mum's place was next door.

Curl up and Dye: Hair and Beauty Salon.

I was glad Sophie's mum's business wasn't boarded up, even though Sophie *had* gone on about me being a class clown and everything. Sometimes you can't stop liking someone, even though you wish you could.

I skimmed round the bench. A tramp sat tipping the dregs from a tin can into his open mouth. I made sure I didn't look him in the eye. Stranger Danger. Always be careful. Always be wary.

The precinct ended and I hit the main road on the other side.

I grew a crampy ache in my side. My trainers rubbed against giant blisters that burnt fresh pain into my sockless heels.

The main road splintered off about fifty yards further on. One road led to school, and the other to the first lot of posh new houses built on the old loony-bin site. I'd never been round there before, but Dad had gone not long after I'd moved in with him. He'd tried to sell his windows to the builder, but the builder hadn't wanted them. He was buying windows for his posh houses from somebody cheaper.

The houses were built on curves and bends and little hills. Neat and clean and smart.

I was still scared about Scuffer and Karl coming after me, but I thought I ought to walk, because running in a posh place can sometimes make you look dodgy.

A rickety wall ran along the back of the gardens. The park woods huddled on the other side, the branches all stretching and scratchy. I tried to ignore the sick lurch in my gut when I thought about walking through the thick of the trees. Well – I wouldn't walk, I'd run. I wouldn't care how dodgy I looked by then. Sneaking glances along the wide curved driveways, I caught glimpses of the crumbly red bricks. I needed to get across that wall, but it was pretty high. You probably needed a high wall to hold loonies in. Ivy tangled over it, and I decided the tangles would make good footholds for climbing.

Every house had a huge garage and a side gate.

Every side gate had a lock.

I walked along, first one way and then the other. I couldn't see any way to get close to the wall.

And then I had the glimmerings of a Plan. The Plan came because of the ginger cat that had nearly had its intestines oozing out. That cat must have belonged to someone. Someone might be wondering where it was. That person might easily go from door to door, asking if anyone had seen it, and I could pretend to be that person. It wouldn't be a very big or terrible lie.

I hurried up the nearest drive and knocked on the first door, but nobody came.

At the second house, the doorbell buzzed like an electric shock. A huge dog bounded down the hall, snarling through the letter box.

I escaped to the third house. Mum always said three was a good number. A lucky number.

The third doorbell rang in a chiming loop, like a lullaby. Soothing. Friendly.

I stood waiting, feeling the sun warm the back of my neck. There was a pink sports car in the drive, and a white butterfly danced all round it as if it thought it was some sort of giant flower.

"Yes?" The lady had cream hair and a cream dressing gown, but her voice was more ice than cream. She was holding a small creamy dog that had round bulgy eyes and a pink bow on its head.

I took a deep breath. "Excuse me, I live just up the road." I waved my hand vaguely, hoping she'd think I was one of her neighbours' sons. "My cat Ginger has run away and Daddy said I should ask if I can look in people's gardens."

Madam Cream narrowed her cold blue eyes. "What's your daddy's name?"

"Um – it's Peter." I got worried that she might know all the neighbours' names. The Plan needed a bit of re-planning. "We don't actually live here but we're staying with Daddy's cousin. He's in the house round the corner."

"I see." Madam Cream raised pencil thin eyebrows and stroked the dog's head. Her fingernails were painted pink. "And your daddy's cousin? What's his name?"

"Er ... John. I think."

I could see through to her kitchen at the end of the hallway. The outside door of the kitchen was wide open, showing off the garden. There were flowers in tubs, and a sprinkler spraying water onto the lawn. I could see the ivy wall running along the back.

My mouth was dry. Mum always said lying made your mouth go dry. Words try to stick to your tongue.

"You don't know your uncle's actual name?"

"We only came last night. It was late. And he's a – a – long lost sort of cousin. Daddy wasn't sure of his name either."

A car was coming down the road and I heard it stop, but it didn't sound rattly and clonked out like Karl Blade's car, so I didn't turn to look.

Madam Cream flicked her gaze past me, shading her eyes. She must have been expecting someone because she said 'At last' in a thin, clipped voice.

And because she was peering past me, and because I knew this was my last ever chance to make the Plan happen, I shoved past her and lurched into her pale pink hall.

The wall was in sight. I just hoped I could get over it somehow.

Only I didn't even get down the hall. I wasn't quick enough. Madam Cream dropped the dog so fast that it yelped. She sprang in after me, grabbing the back of my jacket. I heard more ripping.

"You sneak. You little cheat!" Madam Cream's voice had gone shrill and shaky. The dog gave a yappy bark, snapping my ankles.

I heard car doors slamming.

The sound of heavy boots pounded up the drive. "You're the lady who reported the burglary?"

My heart seemed to drop to my trainers, heavy as a dead cat. The cops!

Madam Cream yanked me round, pushing me in the back and forcing me to face them.

The first copper had a small clipped moustache.

"Yes – I rang about fifteen minutes ago. I don't know

what kept you so long. But you do seem to have come just in time. This little scoundrel has just tried to worm his way into my house again. I expect the villains left some sort of incriminating evidence behind and he's been sent to retrieve it."

The second policeman came closer. He had a turned down mouth which made him look as if he'd been pulling faces when the wind changed.

Tash-man unhooked what looked like a giant mobile from his belt. "What's your name, son?"

I was shaking. Feeling sick again. If I gave Tash-man my name then it would be game over for me and Dad. I'd end up with a police report. A caution or a warning. Mr Snook's file would bulge with notes. He'd stick me back in a foster home faster than Dad could say 'double glazing'.

With a shrug and wriggle I twisted sideways. Madam Cream still had hold of my jacket. I made a sort of ducking movement, stepped forward, then shook my arms out of the sleeves. Scuffer had done me a huge favour by ripping the seam open. The jacket slipped away easily.

I dived past the pink sports car and raced down the drive, dodging the policemen who said "Oi," and "Come back here," but who seemed, just in that second, too surprised to chase me.

I raced out to the road, pausing just once to yell out, "It's not me you want. It's Karl Blade and Scuffer Dobbs. They were in a dented-up silver car earlier. And they've gone round to Scuffer's house. 18 Wesley Road. It's just past the chippie."

I said it because I wanted them to chase off after Karl Blade and Scuffer, rather than me. I didn't really think what Karl Blade and Scuffer would do to me if they found out.

A stupid thing to do.

Sometimes, people you know can bring more danger than strangers.

EARS OF SHAME

I hurried down the long corridor towards the classroom. School seemed, after all, the best option. I could say that I'd been ill, and then overslept. If Miss Kindly rang Dad he'd say it was all true, because it sort of was. Doing spelling tests at lunch break would keep me out of Gabby's reach. So I would get to survive until home time, at least.

With a deep breath I counted to ten, then pushed in through the classroom door.

Miss Kindly was busy at the far side of the room. She had her back to me, so I could sneak in and sit down. Pretend I'd been there for ages.

Everyone was working in groups, chattering in the quiet way that Miss Kindly doesn't mind. Gabby was with Sophie and Jamil. None of them seemed to have noticed me, so I crept along the edge of the room, my shoulders brushing the bookcase. The straw hexagons we'd made in science all wobbled. Two papier mâché puppets slid sideways slowly. Our class globe rocked. Swayed. Then crashed.

I tried to catch it but I have butter fingers. I can never catch anything. Butter fingers and a baked-bean brain.

The quiet chattering stopped.

Gabby nudged Sophie and Jamil in the ribs. "See. I told you."

Every eye turned to me.

"Good heavens, Max." Miss Kindly stared as if I'd just beamed down from another planet. "What are you thinking of?"

Gabby laughed. Others joined in. Soon everyone had a stupid smile stretched across their face. Even Sophie.

I felt my ears flush pink.

"Shhh, all of you." Miss Kindly made her way between the tables and over to me. Her face seemed strange. Almost sad. I wondered if she already knew about the police, and Mr Snook, and all the bad things that might be about to come my way. "Is this another joke, Max? More of your clowning about?"

Puzzled, I looked down to see what she was talking about. And then the horror of the moment hit me. It wasn't just my ears that flushed – my whole body must have flooded redder than a clown's nose.

I was still wearing my too-small-for-me Spiderman pyjamas.

BARE BOTTOM BEAN-BRAIN

I sat slumped on the bed in the medical room.

Miss Kindly hurried in. "Max – so sorry to leave you for so long. I had to get someone to cover." Her face had that 'there there don't worry' expression that grown-ups often gave me.

"There there, try not to worry." Her voice was all sugary. "I've had a chat with the class. No one is going to tease you about this."

Miss Kindly's teasing talk was the worst thing she could have done. Everyone would be kind to me when I went back in. They might even be kind for the rest of the day. But later there would be jokes about pyjama parties. Baby songs and lullabies with the words all changed. Chants made up about my super sexy school uniform.

Miss Kindly gave me a soft smile. "We all do silly things sometimes. You'll have forgotten about it by this time next week. Everyone else will have, too."

My spindly white legs were poking out from my pyjama bottoms. I stared down at them.

Miss Kindly stared as well, and then sighed. "I need to get back to the lesson. I'll send someone down with your PE kit. Then perhaps I should ring your dad? Ask him to come and get you?"

"NO! No." I struggled to grab some sort of control, suddenly not caring how ridiculous I felt. Or how hard it was going to be when I went back in the classroom. "I'm OK. I'm fine."

She put her hand on my forehead. "You don't seem feverish. We'll see how you are at lunch break."

She hurried away again. I wondered if she'd noticed that the sleeves on my pyjama top were too short as well. And two middle buttons were missing. Bits of my flesh pale tummy glinted through.

Was she going to put it all in a report for Mr Snook anyway?

Sophie appeared in the doorway. "Hi, Max. Here's your PE bag."

"Thanks." I couldn't look at her. I kept my gaze fixed on my feet, and wiggled my toes. There wouldn't be any socks in my PE bag, and I hoped Miss Kindly wouldn't suddenly realise I needed some. I'd be forced to wear someone else's stinky cheeses from Lost Property.

Sophie seemed reluctant to leave. She was probably struggling not to giggle. Or, even worse, her face would be as sugary sad as Miss Kindly's had been. Maybe she was feeling sorry for me. Why was I always such a nerd?

I remembered the dreams in the park, and wondered again

if there was something really wrong with me.

"Are you all right, Max? You look sort of lost. Shall I get Miss Kindly again?"

"Yes, I'm all right. No, don't get Miss Kindly," I said.

I took the bag from her, still without looking up.

"Can I help with anything else?"

"No thanks." I waited until she'd left before I slid off the bed. Then I pulled the door shut so no one could see in. Being seen in my too-small-for-me Spiderman pyjamas was bad enough, but giving everyone a flash of my snowy white behind would be even worse.

Bare bottom bean-brain
runs through the town
upstairs and downstairs
with his trousers down. .

THE CHASE

The end of the day came at last. I was the first one pushing out through the school gate.

"Shall I walk with you?"

I glanced over my shoulder and saw Sophie hurrying up behind me.

"If you want." I shrugged. I didn't really care whether she walked with me or not. I wondered whether those cops would still be looking for me.

We trudged without speaking. My trainers made a shushing noise on the pavement. I still didn't have any socks on. My feet would be stinky cheese.

Sophie broke the silence. "I have to help Mum in the salon, so I can't stay with you all the way, but I'll walk with you through most of the precinct."

I knew then for definite that she just felt sorry for me. I didn't want her to. I wanted her to like me and to think I was funny, and to want to hang round with me instead of Jamil.

"You know that thing that happened today, with you

turning up in your jim-jams?"

I pushed my hands deep into my PE shorts pockets. "What about it?"

"Well, I dream about things like that."

"You dream about seeing me in my Spiderman pyjamas?"

"No, silly. I dream that it's happened to me. I turn up somewhere in my undies. Or even worse. It's what's called a 'recurring nightmare'."

I couldn't answer straight away because Sophie had said the word 'undies' and it made my ears flush pink again.

We reached the turn in the road where one way led to the posh new houses and the other way led to the precinct. I stared at my trainers, keeping my head down in case Madam Cream zoomed out in the pink sports car and chased after me. "So what else happens in your dream?" I said at last.

"Usually I'm scared that everyone will look and point and laugh, but just lately I've been trying something new. It's a sort of control tactic. Instead of being at the mercy of whatever happens in the dream, you make yourself aware that it's only a dream even though you're still asleep. Sometimes you can even change what's happening. Make it feel good, instead of scary."

I didn't really get what she was saying, and it wasn't interesting like the bit about the 'undies', but sometimes it's important to be polite. "How d'you do that?"

"You have to practise. My mum's been teaching me. It's actually called lucid dreaming. It's like being awake and watching yourself dreaming."

We were getting near to the precinct. I was sorry Sophie couldn't walk with me all the way home. Gabby had been kept behind by Miss Kindly for sniggering in afternoon assembly, but she might still catch up with me in the park.

"How long do you have to help your mum out for?"

"It depends on what day it is, but today our salon's open till seven, so Mum needs me to help with the twins. Once I get to the salon, she nips off and gets them from the childminder. Then I take them home and make tea. If it's nice, like today, we might go for a walk before bedtime. If not, I read them stories, then do their baths. Mum's usually home just after that."

When I got home I ate crisps and drank Coke. I watched telly or went on my Playstation. I understood more than ever why everybody liked Sophie.

We reached the precinct. It wasn't as bustly as it had been earlier.

Sophie nudged me, murmuring, "Look, there's Scuffer Dobbs. Over on the bench."

I flinched at first because Scuffer wasn't someone I especially wanted to see, but he didn't look as if he was about to cause me any new trouble. He was stretched across the whole length of the bench, his feet hooked over the armrest. The warm sun poured onto his upturned face, burning his nose. He was asleep. "I don't like Scuffer Dobbs very much," I said.

"I don't like him either." Sophie gave a small shake of her head. "He called out disgusting things to Mum when she locked the shop yesterday. She got really scared, especially because he was with Karl Blade and he's *really* bad news. He's been in and out of prison, and he doesn't seem to care. She thought they might try and get the keys off her and trash the salon."

"What about Gabby? D'you like her?"

"Not really." Sophie's voice was thoughtful. "She hangs round me sometimes. I don't mind, but she's not really my friend. I wouldn't invite her round my house or anything. She can be a bit mean. She gets worse when she's with Scuffer."

I wondered if Sophie would ever invite me round her house.

I wondered if Jamil had already been.

I tried to think of a way to make Sophie like me in a 'house invitation' way, and I kept on looking at Scuffer Dobbs.

And then the idea for another brilliant Plan struck me. I strode across to the bench without even stopping to think whether this plan was really any better than the last one. Scuffer Dobbs was snoring. He had hairs in his nostrils and they quivered with each snort. I looked at his sleeping body and I looked at his feet hooked over the armrest. The laces on his trainers were still undone. An accident waiting to happen. I kept watching Scuffer's face and I walked round the bench to be nearer to the trainers.

Grabbing hold of both ends of Scuffer's laces, I knotted them together. And then I tied them again, just to be extra sure.

If I had *just* done that, then everything might have been all right. I could have crept away and gone on walking with Sophie. We could have talked about what he'd do when he woke up. The idea might have made her giggle. She might have begun to like me more.

But the problem was, I didn't creep away. Instead, I poked Scuffer on the shoulder. "Hey, Sleeping Beauty," I said. "Wakey wakey."

Scuffer gave a very loud snort and his nostril hairs quivered more than ever.

"Come on," Sophie whispered. She grabbed onto my arm but I wouldn't go.

"Wakey *wakey*," I called in a sing-song voice.

Scuffer opened one eye. Then he opened the other one. "Ah, it's the Prince of Pyjamas," he smirked in a lazy way. "Glad to see you've got yourself dressed."

He stretched his arms and went to swing his legs down, then frowned. He jerked his legs again, and leant forward to see what had happened.

Scuffer spat some rude words. He spat a lot of them. He shook his fist and tried to punch me, but he couldn't get a swing with his feet tied together.

"Come ON," said Sophie.

This time I did let her pull me away. We chased through the precinct all the way to Curl Up and Dye. "You'd better come inside," she panted. "He's bound to come after you, but I don't expect he'd think to look in here." Her eyes were wide and scared.

I could still hear Scuffer swearing. Looking back, I saw him hobbling towards me.

If I went inside with Sophie, he might hurl a brick through the salon window. He might say more disgusting things to her mum.

"You go in," I said. "I can look after myself." I felt a dizzy sort of fear spin round me as I said it. I hoped I was going to be able to run fast enough. I hurtled out towards the main road. Past the garage and past the chip shop. As I hit the park the dizziness hit me so fast, it was like being spun round. Twizzled like candyfloss round a stick.

And Max was in the tent again.

LIVING MEAT

Max had gold foil stars all round him. A cardboard clown's face leered out. Green hat. Painted eyebrows. Its mouth turned up in a blood-red smirk. Max thought, again, how scary clowns were. Strange and stupid. Fun mixed with fear. He huddled in the corner of the tent, among the crates and barrels.

Sabre lay in front of him, roped loosely to a post that had been dug into the yellowing grass.

George stepped out from the open door of the cage, leaning a rake up against the tent frame. "That's it boy, all clean again for you." He hung a rusted metal key on a hook next to the 'Dance with Death' poster. "Now we can do a spot of training. Brush up on our techniques."

Hunks of red meat were piled up inside the wheelbarrow. A muzz of flies buzzed round it, and a festering stench leaked out. George forked up a slab of meat and carried it across to Sabre, feeding him by hand. The lion took the meat gently. Harmless as a kitten.

"Good chap. Smart chap." He scratched Sabre's ears. Sabre

opened his mouth, and yawned.

Max's mum always said a yawn was a silent shout. Sabre was shouting silently. Max didn't think it was a good idea for George to be scratching the ears of a shouting lion. He remembered the last time he'd been in the tent, when Patches had gone pottering into the cage. He looked round for the crate he'd scrabbled out of, but it was gone.

"Where's Patches?" he called softly.

George turned towards him, grinning with delight. "My ghosted friend returns!"

Max felt his ears flush up. It felt weird having someone who seemed actually *pleased* to see him. He stepped out through the gold foil stars and clown faces. "Is Patches OK? I thought he might be in here. I was hoping to see him again. He makes me laugh." He was babbling, his brain still fuzzy as he got used to being back with George.

"He's out in the woods with Bibi and the chimp. Bibi's completely soft on that puppy. Hardly leaves him for a second." George glanced back at Sabre, then looked at Max again. "I did try to find out about you, but there was nothing in the local graveyard. No record in the church either. Not in births or deaths. Yours can't have been a local family."

"We've only been here six months. I've lived all over the place, and Dad grew up in London."

George studied him carefully. "I'll keep looking," he said at last. "I won't stop until I find you."

Sabre yawned again. George ruffled his mane in the way that Dad sometimes ruffled Max's hair. "Dopey old thing," he said.

Max wasn't sure if he meant Sabre, or him.

George crouched, level with the lion's face. Sabre blinked lazily, then nuzzled his ear.

Scratching the lion's chin, George spoke softly. "Come on, boy, let's show Max your latest trick. Die for the king. Good boy. Die for the king." George's mouth made a whistling shape, although Max couldn't hear anything.

Sabre must have heard something though. He dropped to the ground as if he'd been stabbed. He rolled over. His huge paws were soft. From in between the pads Max saw his claws. Curved and black and sharp.

"I haven't mastered it completely yet, he doesn't do that every time, but I'm getting better and better." George's expression was strangely still, as if he was trying to mask the pride that edged his words. He did the strange, silent whistle again. "Good boy, up now."

Sabre rolled over and sat up, leaning into George. George fed him more meat.

"I don't like teaching him to do that 'die for the king' nonsense, but it's the sort of thing the punters like. And if the punters like it, then the guv'nor will like it. It's the guv'nor I need to convince."

"Convince about what?"

"I want him to give me an act. With Sabre. I want him to let me in the ring."

George stroked Sabre's back and neck. He balled his fists and massaged his shoulders. Sabre butted his head against George's chest, and yawned again.

Could this really be just a dream? It seemed so real. "None of this is real." Max made himself say it out loud, to see how it sounded. "I've just fallen asleep again. There's something wrong with me. I should have let Dad take me to the doctor."

"So you *were* ill." George nodded. "Last time, you couldn't remember how you died."

"I'm not dead." It suddenly seemed important that George should know. "And if *you* were real, Sabre would have eaten you." Max grinned because it felt as if he'd been funny, and clever. A moment of brilliance. And moments of brilliance didn't happen to him very often.

"Big cats – animals like lions and leopards and panthers - are mostly nocturnal. That means they hunt at night. They'll snack a bit by day, but the really serious killer action happens when it's dark – particularly moonless nights."

"Why moonless?"

George shrugged. "They see better in the dark. And probably more to the point, the prey can't see them." George scratched Sabre's ears again. The lion lay down, rested his chin on his front paws, and closed his eyes.

"He might fancy a snack," Max argued. "You said they eat snacks by day."

George jerked his head towards the fly-muzzed meat. "Look at him, he's not even bothered about that banquet. I'm using it as a reward, and he'll take it if I give it, but he's not fussed. But even if he got the tummy-rumbles, Sabre wouldn't eat me. He sees me as part of his Pride – his family, if you like."

"D'you want to be a lion tamer then? Like Danior?"

"Not like Danior. Never like Danior." George's voice grew tight. "But if I can get a decent act together, the guv'nor might just give me a chance."

"Is that your act then? Making Sabre pretend to be dead?"

George shook his head, his voice now almost tight enough to snap. "Not *making* him. Danior *makes* his cats do things, and he does it through fear. I'll never use Danior's whips or heated rods or sticks with spikes."

Sabre's eyes opened. Max saw a flash of the fiery blue he'd seen the first night. The long white tail twitched slowly. He was staring past George and out towards the entrance to the tent.

George shuffled down, resting his head against Sabre's back as if it were a pillow. His voice softened. "I want Sabre to *want* to do things for me. That's the difference between me and Danior."

Max tried to listen, but just in that moment he was caught up watching Sabre's unblinking blue gaze. Perhaps the lion had caught the whiff of a snack outside? He hoped Patches wasn't about to come bounding in. What could Sabre sense? What was holding him so still?

Gradually Max made out a shadow. Someone was outside. Someone was listening. Someone was edging along the front of the tent.

His heart seemed to twist. His throat closed up. "George …" Max's voice felt strangled.

"I've got plenty of other ideas too. I was evacuated to my uncle's farm when all the trouble started. I herded sheep, and learnt to use a special sort of whistling. It was different sounds for different commands, so high pitched that only the dogs could hear. I've tried that whistling on Patches too. He's bright as a button. Responded straight away. So now I'm teaching it to Sabre." George stood up, heading back to the wheelbarrow again. "More meaty treats required."

A rumbling growl trembled in Sabre's throat. George laughed. "Steady boy. I'll be back in two ticks."

"Keep it down, George. I think …"

Max was too late.

The canvas round them billowed, as if a wind had rushed at it. Danior burst into the tent, smacking a punch onto George's chin. George stumbled sideways, knocking against the wheelbarrow as he fell. It toppled, the festering meat sliding slowly as if it were something living. Stinking steaks rolled onto George, half burying him. Scrats of flesh and bone stuck to his collar. The flies buzzed up round it, crawling in his ear.

Danior pulled George to his feet and hit him again. He pushed him backwards up the ramp. George's boots slipped on the metal. One leg buckled under him. Danior kneed him in the groin, grabbing his hair and twisting it.

"Stop it! Leave him!" Max begged.

George groaned. There was blood on his chin. Flies round his mouth.

"You stupid josser." Danior spoke through gritted teeth. "I heard everythin' just now. Dunno who you think you were talkin' to, but it don't matter. Yer intentions are clear. Think you can do a better job than me? Think you can nick my new act?"

He rammed George against the bars of the cage, his hands pressed on his throat.

George's eyes bulged. Fresh blood dripped from his nose.

Max could see he was battling for breath. He lurched forward, thumping Danior on the back of his skull with his useless fists. "You're killing him. You're killing him."

"Big cats. They're in my family. In my blood. And yer just a muck shoveller. A hanger-on cage boy." Danior jerked George's head backwards, thumping it against the bars again.

George kept gasping, his eyes rolling upwards.

"NO." Max kept up his empty thumping. "Don't die, George. Don't die!"

From behind him, Sabre snarled. Max glanced round. The lion was crouching. Ears pricked. Tail flicking. His eyes sparked like living jewels. The rope strained. What if it snapped? Blood smeared George's face, and matted his hair. A piece of living meat.

And Sabre was all animal now. All instinct.

Max turned and kicked Danior. He thumped and punched and battered him.

"Yer bad news for me - and for the whole show. Only a josser would think you can trust a white cat. They're inbred. Makes them more dangerous. Unpredictable. The guv'nor knows that too. That's all part of the punter's delight – the chance to see a good maulin'." He spat the words, then blew out through his teeth, muttering almost to himself now. "I got no problem with the girls – they're too lazy to put up any sort of a fight - but he wants the extra edge from me. So he'll have to work

with me on me own terms. Me own personal safety code."
Danior seemed to suddenly remember George was there. He
wrenched him sideways, dragging him inside the cage. "And
anyway, if you get chewed up by that cat, we're all losers. We
could get closed down. If the guv'nor knew what risks you
were takin' with his precious star-act he'd get you locked up in
that madhouse. Keep you there till the sun burns cold."

George dropped to the floor. He lay curled, his fists covering
his face. Blood oozed from behind his knuckles, trickling into
the sawdust.

Danior slammed the door shut, locking it with the rusty
key. "Yer messin' up that cage. Yer'll 'ave to clean it out again
now. Waste of good litter. Guv'nor should dock that from yer
wages."

George sat up slowly, spitting flies.

Danior stood for a moment longer, looking in at him. "I've
got an expert due to pay a little visit before the end of this
afternoon's show. While I'm enchantin' the punters with the
girls, he'll be givin' yer precious kitty some essential dental
treatment. And a manicure too. You can watch it all. Front row
ticket. I'm sure yer'll enjoy the entertainment."

He dangled the key on one finger, letting it swing for a
moment.

Then he dropped it. It clattered to the bottom of the ramp.

Just out of George's reach.

CAGED

Desperate, Max battled to knock the key to where George could get it. It only needed the tiniest shift. He nudged it. Kicked it. Blew on it. He couldn't even move the specks of sawdust that had drifted and settled either side. "I'm sorry. I'm useless. Completely rubbish."

George sat slumped on the floor of the cage, his head in his hands. "You're a ghost, Max. From another time. You can't change anything here."

"I changed it for Patches. Just by yelling."

"Maybe." George shrugged, and his voice was tired and flat. "I was heading to the cage anyway. I got there a trifle quicker because of you. But who knows, perhaps the pup would have jumped out of the way. Gone back through the bars. We'll never know."

Max looked at him miserably. He hadn't changed things for Patches either then. He really was rubbish.

George's left eye was already bruising. Scabs of blood had dried on his lips, and chin. He kept flicking flies away with weary, irritated swipes.

Sabre paced in uneasy circles round the metal post, his ears flat back. The rope twisted, straining. The post leant dangerously. Max was sure it was only a matter of minutes before it wrenched free completely.

"I'm worried about Sabre," he said. "He's all twitched up and bothered. Look."

At the mention of Sabre, George sat forward. "Settle down, boy. Everything's all right. Gently now."

He pressed his forehead against the bars of the cage, clicking his fingers. "Look at me Sabre. Over here."

Sabre stopped pacing and stared at George. Still uneasy. Tail still twitching.

"Good chap. Good chap. Settle down."

Sabre blinked. He squatted, shook his mane as if he was getting rid of an irritation, then stretched out on the grass.

"You're a genius with him. It's like you've got a magic touch." Max slipped into the cage and crouched beside George. "But what about you? Are you OK?"

George gave a dry laugh. "On top of the world." He rubbed his hair and a soft shower of sawdust sprinkled out.

They sat side by side. Not speaking. Both hugging their knees and watching the now dozing Sabre.

Max broke the silence. "How will that hitman do it?" He wished he'd told George about the hitman earlier. But would that have made any difference either?

"Pliers, most likely. It's not going to be pretty." George's voice was breaking up, and Max could see he was battling tears. "He'll be in agony for weeks. Some cats get their jaws broken. They never properly heal."

Max tried not to think about what it would be like to have your teeth wrenched from your gums. Your nails ripped out. He was battling tears too.

"I hate him. He shouldn't be with cats. He shouldn't be with any animals." George spat out more sawdust, a small splatter of blood mixed up with the spray.

Sabre was sleeping. Twitching slightly. Happily chasing supper in his sleep.

Time passed. Stretched. Seemed endless.

"Maybe someone will come looking for you?" Max tried to make his voice chirpy, but it sounded ridiculous. False and high. Like a teacher insisting *of course* the others would play with you, if you only asked them nicely.

George sighed. "Everyone'll be over at the Top, working at the matinee. Unless they're in charge of a ride, in which case they'll be manning their stall. And they'll all expect me to be cleaning cages. They won't miss me for ages yet."

"Perhaps someone will come to look at Sabre, then? Just by chance?" Max's voice was still in fake teacher mode.

"The guv'nor's twitchy about punters getting a peek at his newest investment. He's planning some sort of summer launch, and wants to build a bit of a buzz, even with his own people. So, apart from myself and Danior, Bibi's the only other one who comes in here - but I've told her to take as long as she wants in the woods. I needed to work on Sabre with nobody around. " George ran his hands backwards through his hair. It stuck up oddly, stiffened with blood. He stretched his legs. Sawdust scuffed up either side of him, making small marks, like soft ripples.

Max did the same – only when he stretched his legs, he made no marks at all. Useless. Rubbish. He could hear the scratched blare of a trumpet, followed by a drumroll. Like distant thunder.

"That's the half-time signal. Still an hour to go." George sighed heavily.

Max wished he could say something helpful. Do something useful. He stared at his legs – his spindly whites - noticing he was in his PE shorts, and vaguely remembering why. He wondered dimly if his real life body was lying flat out in the park? Was Scuffer about to find him? Was Dad driving home early, collecting the burgers? The waking world seemed light years away; it was hard to keep a grasp on the fact that this was really just a dream.

"D'you know what I'd really like?" George's voice broke into his thoughts.

Max frowned, still struggling with fragments of the waking world. "A beefburger?"

"A what?"

"You know – a burger in a bun, with sauce and stuff. I'm hungry."

"Never heard of it. Must be some old fashioned gourmet feast. And anyway, I never knew ghosts had appetites. Trust you to be different." George gave a tired laugh, taking a gentle swipe at Max's head. Max ducked, just from habit. He was an expert at ducking swipes to the head.

They lapsed into silence again. Sabre lay, still dozing. Snoring softly.

"You get a different perspective in here, don't you? Stuck this side of the bars." George squinted as he looked round. "This is what Sabre's world looks like most of the time."

"Don't you ever want to set him free? Give him the chance to just run for his life?"

"It wouldn't be him running for his life. It would be all the punters. All the locals would be tasty human bogie-buns, or whatever it is you call them."

Looking out through the bars had got Max thinking too. He wondered suddenly what Miss Kindly would say. "My teacher says it's wrong to use wild animals for tricks and stuff."

"Everyone uses animals in some way. They ride horses. Keep cats. Breed dogs. And what about those lambs I used to herd? Lovely with mint sauce." George shook his head. "It's important to treat animals with respect, but I don't see how you could stop all that. And if you consider it further, all animals were wild before humans got their greedy mitts on them."

Max couldn't decide what was right or wrong. "But suppose setting Sabre free was the only way to save him from Danior?"

"He's semi tamed now. We can't turn time back for him." George flicked more flies away. "You're right – it's not a perfect life. But it's not a tremendous treat for the humans here either. The whole circus industry is on its knees.

108

Punters just don't want to come any more."

"I heard Danior say that, too."

"Heard Danior say what?"

"He was on about people not wanting to go out because they had special boxes in their houses instead."

George frowned, then gave a short laugh. "Television. That was what he meant. It probably hadn't been invented when you were alive. But these days there's a set-up called the BBC, and they're in charge of moving picture boxes that show entertainment and news stories. My father kept going on about getting one. He always wanted everything, but we couldn't pick up the special transmissions where we lived." George sighed and shook his head. "I keep hearing people talking about it though, and it's my guess that in the future more and more families are going to be sat indoors watching those boxes. There'll be no reason for them to even step outside their cosy front parlours, let alone put their hands in their pockets for tired old circus acts. That's why the guv'nor is so sweet on Danior. He's persuaded Guv'nor that punters will come flocking in to see a rare white lion, and even without Sabre, he needs a big cat act of some sort. He's right too. The posters wouldn't have the same pull without the girls splashed across them."

Max was about to tell him he was wrong about his not being alive when telly was invented. It would clear up the being dead thing completely. But an engine spluttered up round the edge of the tent. Brakes screeched. The engine rumbled like a low growl.

Sabre opened his eyes. Flicked his ears. Stood up and stretched.

"Back up a bit. Get as close to the tent as you can." Danior's voice scuffed out from beneath the snarl of the engine.

George stood up too. He pressed his whole body against the bars, gripping them so tightly the cage rattled. "Looks like the mobile beauty parlour's arrived." His hands were shaking.

The engine coughed, and stopped.

The bars had pressed lines into George's face, striping it with grime and dust and blood.

"Maybe they've changed their minds." Max was suddenly hopeful. "It's all gone quiet out there again."

"No chance. I know how Danior operates. He's probably joined his brutish buddy in the van. He'll be sharing a ciggie with him. Making sure they've both agreed what's what. Making sure there won't be any misunderstandings, or mistakes. He tried all that sort of talk on me at first, until he realised I wasn't going to play ball with him."

Max stood up and shuffled next to George. They stood in silence. Max's gut churned and twisted.

And then, suddenly, there was a distant voice. A child calling. Getting closer. The voice was light. Lilting. A happy melody of sound. "Come on, Patches. Chase the stick."

Max looked at George. "Call her. Shout for her."

George shook his head, murmuring, "No good. The minute I risked a shout, Danior would be in here, shutting me up. The blokes that take out cats' teeth are proper gangsters. Killers. I'd have a good chance of joining you in your ghost world, once they'd finished with me."

George slumped, crouching, still gripping the bars. "Useless," he said hoarsely. "We're both useless."

"Both rubbish," added Max, crouching too. And then suddenly an idea exploded in his head. His second moment of brilliance that day. "Those dogs you were going on about. On your uncle's farm …"

"What about them?" George's voice was empty.

"You said you'd taught them a special whistle. Something only they could hear."

"They're about two hundred miles away. Even my whistles aren't *that* special. And anyway, what good would it do if they were?"

"You taught it to Patches too. You said so earlier."

"So what?"

"If you whistle for Patches, he'll come running to you. And you said Bibi hardly leaves him for a second …"

"Max - you're a genius. What a wasted life, you dying so young." George stood up again, and whistled. A pitch so special, Max's ears couldn't hear.

THREAT

It was a drumroll moment of triumph. Danior and his hitman burst in to find George forking up the spilled meat. Bibi sat near the gold foil stars, trying to see if Patches 'liked butter' by waving a yellow petal under his chin. Patches chewed her fingers. She giggled, tickling him. He rolled over for her to scratch his tummy, ears flopping inside out.

"Don't squish me flowers. You knows they're a present for Ma." Bibi giggled again. But she scratched his tummy anyway, and Patches squirmed round and licked her face, his stumpy tail wagging madly.

Sabre was back in his cage, rubbing his mane against the bars.

The hitman stopped when he saw Bibi. She smiled shyly at him.

"Georgie locked hisself in Sabre's cage. He were cleanin' him out, and dropped the key. Silly Georgie," she said.

"Very silly indeed." Danior was two paces behind the hitman, and for a moment Max didn't recognize him. He wore a black sequined waistcoat. Tassled white trousers.

Heavy black boots. But he looked at George and his eyes were daggered. Still the same Danior on the inside.

"Luckily Bibi came in just a few minutes ago, and handed me the key." George grinned at Bibi. "She's a clever girl."

Bibi glowed pink with pride. "George hurted his face on the rake. I used Sabre's water to help him clean the ouchy bits." She stopped tickling Patches and he twisted round, gnawing the side of her hand. She lifted him high, then rocked him like a baby. "Naughty Patches," she murmured.

"I don't work in front of kids. We agreed we might need this cage-boy to keep the cat calm, but you said no one else would be around." The hitman made his gobby spitting noise again. "You said I'd get the job done without anyone snooping about."

Danior daggered another look at George. George grinned and winked at him. Max grinned and winked at him too, even though he knew Danior couldn't see.

The hitman began backing out of the tent. "Call me some other time. When you're not running a nursery."

"We're here all week. I'd have to find a way to shut this josser up, but if yer around Friday …?"

"Got a job up near home, in London. Won't be back for a few days now."

"We're travellin' on to West Hollow, settin' up there on Sunday. I'll sort a new date for then."

"No chance. There's a young lady in West Hollow I wouldn't want to risk meeting, if you get my meaning." The hitman was already gone. His footsteps thudded as he humphed back to his van. A door opened. Slammed. The tyres seemed to stick for a moment, screeching against the roar of the engine. Then the sounds faded as he drove away.

George and Danior didn't move. The air seemed thick with a silent ticking. Both of them waiting for the bomb to go off.

And then Danior spat. He stormed over to George, kicking the pitchfork from his hands. "Yer'll regret this. I'll find a way to get back at you. To get rid of you permanently."

George faced him. "Not if I find a way to get rid of you first."

The two of them glared. Anger pulsed through the veins in their necks.

Max trembled, thinking the fight would start up again. "Leave him, George," he said softly. "He's not worth it."

"No more crossness, you two," whispered Bibi, hugging Patches tightly. "Please."

None of them saw Patches slip out of Bibi's arms. He pottered over to where George and Danior stood. Their eyes stayed locked together. Their fists were clenched and ready.

They still didn't notice the puppy.

Not until they heard the thin trickle of water.

Patches was widdling on Danior's left boot.

FALLING

Danior stood still as the widdle dripped down the side of his boot. A small puddle pooled in the grass. Max waited for the explosion. Waited for Patches to be kicked or hurled to the other end of the tent.

"Don't be all grumpity with Patches." Bibi tiptoed over and tugged Danior's sleeve. "He's ever such a good puppy really."

From across the park, the trumpets started up again.

Danior looked down at Bibi, jerked his arm away, then strode out of the tent.

"Silly Patches," said Bibi softly, bending and picking him up again. "It's not safe to make Danior cross." She looked up at George and her eyes glistened. "I'm frighted he might put Patches in a sack with rocks and drop him in a river. Like what he's did before."

George knelt down until his face was level with hers. He touched her left cheek very gently with one finger. "He'll calm down. He's gone off to do his turn in the ring, and who knows – he might be all smiles if he gets a good response from the audience. He might come back so happy you end up with a kitten and a pony and a … a … a cuddly tiger cub to train for when you're bigger."

Bibi stared at him with wide, hopeful eyes. "I could train a big cat? Be like Danior when I gets growed up?"

"Better than Danior. Better than anyone." George glanced at Max, who nodded enthusiastically, wishing he could join in with ideas for her wonderful future .

"Come on." George grinned and held out one hand to her. "Let's treat ourselves to a ride at the fair. Anything you choose. But you'd better go and give those flowers to your Mum first, and see if she'll take care of Patches for a while." He turned to Max and tilted his head, one eyebrow raised in question.

It took Max a moment to realise George didn't just mean himself and Bibi. He meant all three of them.

They stepped out of the tent, and into the late afternoon. The air was warm. Sweet scented. A few clouds drifted like candyfloss, nudged by a quiet breeze that Max couldn't feel. The roundabout horses rose and fell. Two girls slid, laughing, down the helter skelter. A wobble-wide woman blew a kiss to Bibi from behind a coconut stall. "Come an' win a prize, sweetheart. Anything you fancies."

Bibi giggled and blew her a kiss back. "I will later. Promise or die. But just now I has to go an' see Ma."

The roller coaster gave three shrieked blasts as it hurtled along the track. They passed the clown-shoot, and Max saw, to his relief, that the back shelf wasn't stashed with pickled body-parts in jars. They were fish. A woman in a white jacket had just won one. She held it up, and it flashed gold where the sunlight caught it, glowing like a swimming flame. "I'll get a pond dug in the garden for this little chap. Reeds and lilies, and ferns round the edge." She smiled, and wandered away.

Bibi skipped ahead, still holding Patches. He had his head on her shoulder, his eyes half closed. His ears flopped and bounced as she ran, disappearing between the trailers.

George turned, murmuring to Max. "I want you to have a good time too. As normal as we can manage."

A woman with heavy gold earrings sat inside a stall. Sun-yellow ducks bobbed up and down in a trough of water.

"Afternoon, Rosa. I'll try my hand at this." George fished in his pocket for some change.

Rosa handed George a stick, with what looked like a metal claw on the end.

George grabbed a duck easily. "Beginner's luck," he grinned.

"Be grateful for any sort of luck, sweetheart." Rosa smiled back. "You can choose yer prize from these." She waved her hand at a string of soft toys that hung inside the stall.

"I'll take one of those brown bears, please. The bottom one. He looks friendly."

Rosa cut it down, and handed it to George. He turned, tossing it at Max. "Catch."

Max stretched to grab it, but it slid through his hands. Dropped to the grass.

"Oh blast. I forgot you couldn't - you know, touch anything. I'm getting so used to you. You seem so real."

"You don't want it?" Rosa jangled her jewelled wrist at George. "I'll put it back on the stall and you can 'ave somethin' else."

George picked the bear back up and looked at it for a moment. "No, Rosa," he said slowly. "I'm going to keep it. It's going to remind me of a special sort of friend."

He tucked it inside his jacket and winked at Max. Max winked back, washed by a rush of happiness. A silly sort of happiness that seemed strangely close to crying. George had just called him a friend again.

Bibi came racing over. "Patches were fast asleep when I got to our wagon, so I left him all snuggled up with Clover. Ma's sat outside stitchin' costumes, so she said she'll just stay with him till I gets back."

"Shall we head over to the roller coaster then? It's the best ride here." George was murmuring, talking from one side of his mouth. Max realised the question was for him.

He answered back from one side of his mouth too. "I'm not good with rides like that. Remember I told you I honked up on the last one I went on?" Max looked across to where the 'haunted' train waited at the beginning of the ride. Loobrush sat by the ticket booth, counting coins and muttering to himself. "And anyway, I wouldn't be able to hold on to the bar. What if I fell out?"

"Well, it won't kill you. That's one advantage." George grinned.

"I don't want to do it. I'd hate it."

George did the one eyebrow thing, and nodded. "Fair enough. Let's do the Ferris wheel. D'you feel safe about that?"

And minutes later all three of them were being lifted gently upwards.

Max pressed himself into the narrow bench seat, still half believing he might slip out. How would he fall? Would he float? Would it be like flying? Or would he wake up and realise he was hurtling towards a messy ending?

The sweet peachy smell grew fainter as they rose higher.

Everything seemed slowed down. Dreamy. Timeless. Even the horror of the fight in the tent slipped away.

"Look." George pointed across the fields. A church steeple rose up in the distance. "That's West Hollow over there. It's where we're going next. I hope this weather lasts. The guv'nor's pinning his hopes on our pulling in a good crowd for this coming Saturday. It's our last day here, and we'll get more punters if the sun keeps shining."

Max's gaze followed where George was pointing. He knew vaguely where West Hollow was. There were signs to it up by the main road, but he'd never been there.

The church bell tolled six solemn dongs, the sound rolling through the quiet blue sky. He'd never heard it ring before. He'd never even seen the steeple. In his real-time world there were too many buildings in the way. And probably too much noise.

A hot-air balloon floated past, the sudden blast from its

burner making Max jump. "Archie! Archie! Look at me and Georgie up near the clouds. Over here!" Bibi waved frantically at the peak capped pilot, but he had his back to her and didn't look round.

The passenger saw her, though. It was the white jacketed goldfish woman. She lifted her hand and smiled as the balloon drifted by. It rose higher. Changing course. Sailing away until it was just a dot in the distance.

The trumpet and drum noises seemed muffled and far away. The Ferris wheel started and stopped. Started and stopped. Each time edging them upwards.

Max craned his neck round, trying to glimpse the view through the other side. He could make out turrets. A wall. But they weren't right at the top yet, and the Ferris frame blocked his view. He told himself it would be OK. He'd see it all properly in a minute. But his gut began to churn with a new anxiety. What *would* he see? And if it did turn out to be the old asylum, still standing, what would it mean?

"Show's finished, look." George made a nudging movement with his elbow. "I haven't got long. I'll have to go and sort the girls out before the evening performance."

Max could make out the Big Top - red and gold – a thin flag fluttering lazily. A straggle of people spilled out from one end of the marquee. He saw Martha being led away from over at the far side, rolling a fat, striped ball along with her trunk. A string of white ponies trotted past her, purple feathers bobbing between their ears.

And from further back still, the guv'nor appeared. The

tall black hat graced his head. The same gold-trimmed red jacket. White gloves. Long boots. He stood, watching the straggled people walk away. If he'd been thinking they'd head for the rides that hooted and whirled, he was wrong. Most of them moved steadily towards the gate. The guv'nor kept watching even when they were gone, and just for a moment his shoulders sagged. As if everything was too tiring. Or too pointless. And then he shrugged. Straightening up, he strode towards the fair, tipping his hat and smiling at the few visitors who'd stayed on.

Bibi began singing to herself, rocking slightly. A soft gypsy lullaby with words Max couldn't recognize. He was glad she was happy, and he let himself relax, listening to the lilt and flow of her little-girl voice.

And then, Max saw someone hovering behind the guv'nor – someone in a sequined black waistcoat, all glittery in the sunlight. "There's Danior." Max leant forward and squinted. "Does he use that whip?"

"He's got torture tools much worse than that. The girls aren't lazy. They've closed down. Dulled by too much fear." George was watching him too.

Max saw the guv'nor turn and see who was behind him. He saw him listening. Shaking his head. Touching Danior on the shoulder, as if he was trying to calm him down. "Looks like the two of them get on pretty well."

"That's because the guv'nor never sees the worst of him."

Bibi stopped singing and cuddled into George. "What you sayin', Georgie?"

"Sorry, Bi – just admiring the view out loud." He turned back to Max, murmuring, "I wish I knew what they were saying though. I bet my name's being dragged through all manner of mud."

Max nodded. He was pretty sure that was exactly what Danior was up to. They were getting close to the highest point of the ride, but suddenly, Max forgot about watching for the madhouse, and the brick wall, and whatever other weirdness might come looming. "I can go over there," he said. "Listen in. Report back."

George gave a heavy sigh. "It would be incredible if you could. I could find out exactly what sort of knives he's stabbing me in the back with. But this thing chunters round at a snail's pace." He rocked the car with sudden frustration. "Whatever muck Danior's spreading about me, he'll have spread it by the time we get to the bottom."

Max looked at the frame of the Ferris wheel. "It's a bit like a ladder," he said slowly. "Not really dangerous. And anway, I'll probably float through it." His heart was banging. His mouth dry.

"You mean to say you'd risk jumping? Just for me?" George shook his head. "You never would. You wouldn't even go on the roller coaster five minutes ago."

And it was something in those two sentences that made Max straighten his back. He *would* do it for George. To help him out – and to show George that he wasn't really a wimp. He wanted George to feel proud of knowing him, in the way that he was proud of knowing George. "Watch me," he said.

"You said earlier one advantage of my falling would be that I wouldn't die."

And before he could change his mind, he was standing up. Trying not to see the space underneath him. Swallowing down the giddy fear that seemed to stick in his throat.

"Look, Max – I truly don't think you should risk it. We don't have any idea what might …"

Max stepped out of the car.

There was a panicked, frozen moment as he scratched the air. The frame of the Ferris wheel creaked round. Roared in his head. And he knew in that last second that George was right. He shouldn't have risked it. He was rolling, turning, tumbling down and down and down. The ground rushed to meet him. He braced himself for the greatest agony ever. Somewhere above him, George was yelling his name.

"I'm sorry," Max sobbed. His mouth stretched strangely and his tongue was too big. "I surrrry. Surrry surry surrrry."

And a man's voice said, "Nothing to be sorry about, Max; we're here to take care of you."

"Shall I go round and tell his dad? I know where he lives?" Sophie was standing with the twins. They clung to her, staring at me as if I was a three-headed monster.

The late afternoon sun shimmered along the railings round the edge of the park.

Scuffer leant on the gate, drumming his fingers. There was an ambulance parked up next to him, its back doors wide open.

My words were still stumbling. My brain trying to catch up. "My daddy dada probably burgy buying. Home not there. Anyone."

"No problem, Max." The ambulance man took hold of my arm. "Can you walk all right? You can lean on us if you need to."

A second ambulance man stepped forward and gripped me from the other side. He raised a hand to Sophie. "Well done for ringing us, Miss. You did the right thing. And thanks for staying until we got here. He might have done himself an injury."

They led me across the grass and out through the gate. I stumbled, but the ground stayed firm beneath my feet. Solid.

Scuffer watched my every step, a thin leer across his face. Then he turned and walked away. Very slowly. Turning back to stare at me again after every few steps. *You'd better watch out*, his slow walk said. *I'm not going far.*

"Just up here, Max." The two men led me up the ramp. "We're going to sit you down on the bed. That's right. Well done. Good lad."

My hands were shaking and I kept blinking. Rubbing my eyes. Looking up just before the doors closed, I saw Sophie staring in at me as if I was some sort of loony. She was probably right.

CABBAGE BRAIN

They stuck me in a ward on my own. I spent most of the next day staring blankly at the ceiling, trying to make sense of what was happening to me. Nurses came and went, checking charts and smiling. A group of doctors came too, huddling round the bed, muttering doctorish words that sounded like another language.

The bed was by a window, and from time to time, when I couldn't bear the muddle of my own thoughts, I gazed outside instead. A big town sprawled out far below. Grubby grey buildings and a mash of roads. Closer in, I could count the cars in the car park. Watch people come, and go. Milling about like ants. There were more hospital buildings too. One had a flat roof, and a hurrying nurse told me that sometimes a helicopter landed there. She said it while a thermometer was rammed in my mouth, so I couldn't ask any questions.

I kept watching for a helicopter after that. None came.

I was still there in the evening. Another nurse, wearing a sort of blue bin liner apron, wheeled in a fish pie and orange jelly on a trolley. "Hello there, Max. Dinner time."

"Thanks." I waited till she'd gone, forced down two mouthfuls of the pie, and slurped up the jelly. Then I pushed the tray away.

The sky outside grew dusky. It was too early for stars.

"You must be a Very Important Patient." Dad appeared in the doorway. "You've still got this room all to yourself."

"They probably think I'm dangerous."

I'd had an X-ray earlier, and a blood test, and a nurse with flame-red hair had whispered secrets to a white-coated Doctor Koff. The secrets were about me. The secrets told him I'd been found stumbling around, shouting and waving my arms about. Doctor Koff muttered things like 'narcolepsy' and 'sleep disorder'. He wrote notes on a sheet of paper and hung it on the end of my bed.

I told him I'd had weird dreams and I'd felt a bit dizzy. I mentioned sometimes feeling blurry and muddled, and not being able to talk right. I didn't tell him much else. I didn't want him to realise how weird I really was. I was keeping secrets too.

Dad sat down on the white plastic visitor's chair, and handed me an envelope as big as my hospital pillow. "One of your friends' mums dropped this round just as I was leaving to come here. I'm not sure of her name, but it's the woman that runs that hair salon place in the precinct."

The card inside had an umbrella on the front:

HEARD YOU'RE FEELING

UNDER THE WEATHER

I opened the card and a sun popped out.

HOPE YOU'RE YOUR
SUNNY SELF AGAIN SOON

Miss Kindly

Everyone from my class had signed it. Some had written jokes:

Who invented hospital gowns?
- answer -
Seymour Bottom

Doctor, Doctor, I think I'm a bell.
Take these and if they don't help,
give me a ring.

Doctor, Doctor, I think I've got wind!
Can you give me something for it?

Yes, here's a kite ...

Sophie hadn't written a joke. She'd drawn petals all round the 'a' part of my name and said she hoped I'd get better soon.

Jamil wrote,

'Sincere good wishes'.

Gabby's bold writing stood out from all the rest.

'can't wait to see you again !'

She'd written with a red felt pen, and added drippy blood shapes underneath the exclamation mark.

I dropped the card down onto the bed, and stared back out through the window again. I was still hoping for a helicopter. "I must have looked really stupid in the park."

"Don't worry about it, mate," said Dad. He sounded worried. "It doesn't matter."

"It does matter." My voice came out sulky. "Can we move away from here? Go to a different town?"

"Don't be daft, Max mate. We've only just about got settled. And look how many friends you've got. Look how much they care about you." He picked the card up, and did some fake window-seller laughing at the jokes.

I stared at my knees. They looked like camel humps under the sheets.

Dad put the card on a small white cabinet next to my bed. He smiled his window-seller smile at me. I remembered Sophie's face as she'd stared inside the ambulance and wished I could curl up and die.

The flame-haired nurse came bustling across. "Good evening, Mr Baxter. We've done some tests and Max's having a final scan in about half an hour, to check for abnormal brain activity. Doctor Koff will talk you through the finer detail. He's dealing with another patient at the moment, but I'll let him know you've arrived."

I didn't like the idea of being checked for 'abnormal brain activity'. There was a boy on telly once who had something wrong with his brain. He'd gone into a coma, and never come out. The reporter on the programme said he'd be a vegetable for ever.

I pictured myself as a giant cabbage plonked in the middle of the hospital bed. Would anyone send cards to a cabbage? The nurse bustled away.

"Ah hello, hello. Mr Baxter, I presume?" Dr Koff strode in from the corridor and shook Dad's hand. He had tufty grey hair and goldfish bowl glasses, and he peered at me from over the tops of his lenses. "There are several possibilities, but the scan will help us to be more certain. I'm more inclined to lean towards the sleep disorder options. I'd like to refer Max to a specialist once we've discharged him from here. They'll do tests on the brain function during sleep."

"D'you think it might be something serious?" Dad had

his knuckles pressed against his mouth.

Dr Koff glanced at the notes again. "Based on the information I have, I'm tempted to diagnose a condition called 'narcolepsy'. Sufferers tend to fall asleep at any time. Even when they're standing up. But it's early days. We mustn't jump to conclusions." He took a pen from his top pocket and jotted down something new.

So it was definite then. A medical explanation. George and the others were all just dream-land characters. I felt achingly sad. I missed them all. Even Sabre – but especially George. He was the closest thing to a friend I'd ever had.

I looked out of the window again. Still no helicopters.

"The nurse will organise an outpatient appointment at the sleep clinic. In the meantime, keep a diary and make a note of any unusual sleeping patterns, vivid dreams, dizzy spells or fainting fits."

A buzzer sounded from somewhere outside, along the corridor.

Dr Koff jolted backwards, as if he was on a string and someone had just pulled it. "I'm afraid I must go. I'll ask the nurse to come and complete the paperwork." He hung the notes back on the end of the bed, and rushed away.

Minutes later, the flame-haired nurse hurried in and plumped up my pillow. "The doctor doesn't think there's any danger, so we should be able to get you discharged tomorrow morning. You can spend the rest of the week at home, being fussed over. No school for a few days. That's the good side of all of this." She beamed like someone holding out a cuddly teddy to a toddler.

I threw a panicked glance at Dad. "My dad can't stay off work!" I was thinking about Mr Snook.

Dad interrupted. "Shhhh, Max. Don't worry. I expected this, and it's all sorted."

"But Dad - you mustn't."

"Is there a problem?" The nurse frowned. She had picked up the sheet, and looked ready to scribble more notes. Mr Snook and the nurses and Dr Koff would all like each other. They'd like whispering secrets together.

"No problem at all." Dad fixed me with his fiercest 'don't interrupt' expression. "It's a bit hard for me to take time off at present, but Max is very lucky. Our neighbour is elderly so she doesn't work, and she's offered to have him in with her. It's just for two days – until the weekend."

My mouth opened and closed but no sounds came out. I was as trapped as a goldfish in a jar.

"Max gets on very well with her. He'll be very happy, won't you, Max?" Dad's eyes were still locked onto mine. I knew there wasn't any choice.

I looked away. It had grown dark outside. The silver moon stared coldly in through the window. There were still no helicopters. A dark-winged bird flapped across the night sky. Another chant flapped across my mind.

Barmy Barbara's brains a sponge
made from toads and
frogs and gunge
Barmy Barbara's baggy pants
crawl with itchy witchy ants

SLUG-SLIME

I stood awkwardly in the front room. The closed curtains were a shabby green. An ancient lamp glowed from the furthest corner. A bundle of rags, some scissors and the wicker basket she'd been carrying in the park were on the table beside it.

There were cats everywhere. On the backs of chairs. Under the table. A brown striped one sat perched on Barbara's shoulder.

The cats watched me with their slanty yellow eyes. "How many cats have you got?" I didn't look at Barbara when I spoke. I didn't want to see her scar.

"Seven. Thistle's asleep on my bed upstairs. She's a little bit poorly so she's had some herby milk. It's calmed her down a lot, but she gets cross if she's woken." Her voice was quivery. Wheezy.

There was a gold patterned vase on the windowsill, and pale yellow flowers shielded a folded, official looking piece of buff-coloured paper. The whole room stank of the peachy sweet scent, mixed with cat wee. "I didn't even know you had cats."

"I don't let them out, dear. I worry about all the cars." Barbara hobbled round the room, making clucking noises at the cats. They stretched their necks and gazed at her. "They're not used to visitors. I need to let them know you're not going to hurt them." She kept muttering, stopping by a small ginger one and picking it up. I wondered why she'd agreed to look after me.

How would I survive a whole day? I'd have to watch endless telly. Only, I suddenly realised I couldn't actually *see* one anywhere. "Where's your telly?" I was trying to sound polite, but was panicking slightly. *What if she didn't have one?* It's hard to sound polite about something as important as a missing telly.

Barbara rested beside a tattered green armchair. "My family were against them. And the nurses didn't permit details about the outside world to be watched by their patients. They always told us we'd find it too distressing. I grew up without ever knowing what television was."

I boggled a look at her, just from the shock. Her one foggy eye peered anxiously back. Her hair fell across the side of her face. I was grateful for the falling hair, because it hid the scar.

I'd been scared of the scar all night long. I'd lain in bed thinking about it, and later dreamt it sort of wiggled off her face and attacked me. A nightmare of nightmares. I woke up shouting, bashing the air. A tired eyed nurse had hurried in to check I was OK.

Barbara began stroking the ginger cat. It gazed up, making a burry noise in its throat. Barbara's fingers were bone thin. Mottled brown. Like twigs.

I knew I had to say something quickly, to try and explain my shocked staring. "I hated hospital," I managed at last. I couldn't think of anything better to break the moment.

"I was very unhappy when I was in one, too." A black and white cat slipped out from under the table and padded over to her, rubbing itself against her legs. "You do get used to unhappy things though, dear. I lived there for a long, long time."

I stayed standing, still awkward. There was a hole in my sock and my big toe poked out, but Dad had made me promise to take my trainers off when I got in the house. He'd said Barbara wasn't used to clod-hopping boys trampling about. He'd said she was doing us both a big favour, and I had to show respect. He'd said all that after quizzing me about what had happened to my jacket, although in fairness he didn't have a go for long. Which was just as well, because I didn't know if the story I'd stammered out about losing it in the park some time before the ambulance came, would hold up.

"Couldn't your family have moved you to a different hospital, if you were miserable for so long?" I was trying to be polite again.

"I'm afraid I never saw them."

"What d'you mean?"

"I waited and waited for them to come and take me

home, but they never did. They never even visited."

"They must have rung. Or written."

"Neither of them could write, dear. And they wouldn't use a telephone either. They believed all the new inventions were dangerous."

I decided Barbara's family must have been as barmy as her. She gave me her sad, twisty smile.

"So how did your family keep in touch, to check you were OK?"

"They didn't, dear. I never heard from them again. Not until last week anyway." Barbara seemed to be talking to herself now. Almost whispering. "It turned out my brother was in a care home. And he wanted to see me. One of the nurses sent me a letter."

"What did he want to see you about?" I struggled to catch what she was saying.

Barbara plucked at the sleeve of her baggy green cardigan. "I'm afraid I don't know. The nurse said he was very agitated. Very unhappy. It made me feel sad for him, but I really couldn't go. The care home is a long way away and I wouldn't have had anyone to look after the cats. I've lived here a very long time, but I've never got to know any of the neighbours."

I felt sorry for her then, and wondered if she knew about all the witchy chants.

Barmy Barbara
bird's nest hair
squiggly wiggly
worms in there

"You could call your brother now. I've got my mobile." I pulled it out of my jeans pocket, feeling suddenly buzzed up. Keen to find out what he wanted to tell her. And at least it would be something to do, to kill the telly-less eternity.

Barbara's one eye boggled at the mobile as if she thought it might be about to leap out of my hand and bite her. Then she shook her head, hunching forward as if she was in some kind of pain. "He died last week. The funeral was Monday, but I couldn't go there either. They sent me a copy of the death certificate, and a 'with sympathy' card. I'm a little ashamed to say I threw the card away, but I propped the certificate against the flowers there. It seemed like the right place to put it."

I glanced across at the folded, official looking paper, and wondered again what her brother had been so desperate to see her about. Maybe it was to say sorry for never visiting? Or perhaps there was a grisly deathbed secret he needed to blurt out with his dying breath? But then again, it was probably more to do with warning her about the vile evils of computers, and barmy-brained nonsense like that.

I was cheesed off with Dad.

He'd said I had to stay round Barbara's. He'd said it would be rude to make her spend the day round ours. But he hadn't mentioned the whole lack of telly thing. What did they expect me to do all day? I wondered if you could be poisoned by inhaling the stink of cat wee. If Doctor Koff knew what I was being subjected to, he'd send an army of hurrying nurses to rescue me.

A fat black cat jumped onto the windowsill. Its tail knocked against the vase, and the flowers seemed to shiver. A soft scatter of petals floated down onto the stained green carpet. "Careful now, Blackberry." Barbara shuffled over to him, stroking his head and fussing with the flowers. "I know I was wrong to have picked these, but they only grow this time of year. False Oxlips – sometimes known as Ladies' Fingers, I believe. The smells bring back such happy memories. And now my brother's gone ..." her shoulders drooped, "... I seem to need those memories more and more." She hobbled across the room again, steadying herself on the chair next to me.

I wasn't keen on hearing her talk about Ladies' Fingers. It made me think about hubbly bubbly body-bit stews again. But I knew it was only polite to say *something*. I was about to witter on about memories being hard to keep alive, so I turned to face her – and froze. The shock was so huge I almost screamed.

Her witchy hair was snagged up behind her ear. I could see the scar! It ran from where her missing eye should have been. It zigzagged down her neck, all silver. Like slug slime. Other bits were bumpy. Rubbery as egg white. There was a ragged, patched pattern where the stitches had been. Blotches of pinky red lumps spread down across her neck. I thought I might throw up. It was so close. I could have lifted my hand and touched it. And then I remembered Gabby Dobbs and the others making vomit noises whenever they saw me.

I was as bad as them. Worse than them.

Miss Kindly always says you should face your fears. She says facing your fears makes you a stronger person.

I made myself stare into Barbara's foggy eye. The eye stared back. She was trying to hypnotise me. Put a spell on me. I ought to scream, and run.

Face your fears. Face your fears. And then, suddenly, there came a loud hammering at the front door.

WITCH-HUNT

Dad stood on the doorstep, holding a telly. "Just scratted this from the tip. I've got an aerial for it too. Is it OK to fix it up somewhere, Barbara?"

She plucked at her sleeve again. "I'm afraid I'm not sure how they work."

"I'll sort it – but not down here. Have you got a spare room upstairs? That way Max's out of your way. You can still have peace and quiet, even with a galumphing great boy in the house."

He winked at me, and I grinned back. He'd noticed the whole missing telly trauma. He was doing his best for me.

"The spare room is rather cluttered, I'm afraid."

Barbara really seemed to think I might be bothered by muck and muddle, so I chipped in hurriedly, "It'll be great." I grinned at her. "Clutter will make it feel more like my own room."

"Definitely," said Dad. "Clutter is Max's favourite environment."

"Are you … are you quite sure?" Her voice was more

quivery than ever.

I nodded, my head bobbing like an enthusiastic seal. "Quite sure."

"I'll lead you to it then." Barbara hobbled to the stairs, the cat still on her shoulder. "It's the main bedroom. The one at the front of the house. I've never felt happy sleeping so close to the road."

Dad followed, lugging the telly, while I trooped behind holding the plug lead and aerial.

"This is it." She creaked open a cobweb laced door, and we all trailed in.

"It's brilliant," I forced the words. Forced a smile. At least it didn't stink of cat wee. There were no curtains, so the sunlight washed in, lighting patchwork cushions and blankets, all squashed between a jumble of furniture.

"Maybe it really isn't … if you'd be kind enough to just give me five minutes I could try and …" Barbara was wavering again.

"You get back to doing whatever you do in the morning." Dad beamed her the fakest window-selling smile I'd ever seen. "Max can help me."

She nodded at last, plucked at her sleeves, then hobbled off again.

Dad had the telly working in less than twenty minutes. "There's no remote, mate, but you just mess about with these knobs. You should be able to get at least two channels from it." He ruffled my hair, then looked at his watch. "I've got to dash – I just grabbed a gap between appointments, but I'll nip back again at midday, just to check you're OK. You stay here, and I'll let Barbara know I've gone. "

Five minutes later, I was standing in the spare room next to Barbara, who'd shuffled back in to 'see me settled'.

"I'll pop up from time to time to see if you want anything, dear. Remember your dad said you're not to risk walking down the stairs on your own."

Cheers, Dad! He'd gone a bit loony himself over this whole narcolepsy thing. I was lucky he wasn't insisting she watched me go to the loo. "Thanks. That'll be great." I wanted her to go. I couldn't bear this endless, awkward business of being polite. I couldn't bear the old lady smell of her. And even though I knew it was wrong, I still couldn't bear being near the scar.

She must have sensed my thoughts, because after a moment she made a funny, wheezy little sigh, then left me alone. I heard her murmuring something to the cat, the stairs creaking as she hobbled down. Soon there was the clatter of pots and pans being moved about in the kitchen. And a croaky, raspy noise that must have been Barbara singing. I tried not to think about the body-bits stew.

Dad had set the telly up on an ancient dressing table. The glass on the mirror was smeared with grime. I looked in at my reflection.

I was blurred. Like a ghost. Did dreams carry on when you weren't dreaming them?

I plonked myself down on the sofa and turned the telly on. It was crackly at first, the screen all fuzzy. I had a panicked moment thinking I might have to sit goggling at the crackles till lunchtime – but then a picture came up. A yawn boring programme about buying a house.

I played with the knobs, and found a war documentary thing. All black and white. Bomber planes screamed through a night sky. A wrinkly woman wittered on about driving an ambulance. A sad faced bloke held up a crumpled photo of his house before the Blitz. He kept stroking the edges, as if he was trying to flatten it out and make the picture new again. Turn back time. I'd heard of the Blitz. Miss Kindly showed us an olden days film about children going to live in the country so they wouldn't get blown up. I wondered what Barbara had done? Perhaps she'd got her scar from an exploding bomb? The programme finished, just as Barbara rattled in with an old wooden tray. The brown striped cat lay draped over her shoulder like a scarf. I wondered, for one brief, bold moment, whether to actually ask her about her scar. Just blurt out the question.

But she spoke first. "I've brought you some nice sandwiches, dear. And … and I've made biscuits too. I hope you'll like them. I'm afraid I wasn't sure what boys eat."

"Thanks." I beamed out my own fake smile. I hated sandwiches. I'd rather munch on cardboard. I knew I wasn't showing respect, but the thought of eating stuff Barbara had *actually touched* made me feel vomity again.

*Barmy Barbara
boils bats' bladders
nibbles newts
and eyes of adders*

I took the tray from her, hoping she wasn't going to sit and watch me eat. There were cat hairs on my plate. I pictured Blackberry plonking his fluffy bottom down on the sandwich.

"Your dad agreed earlier it would be safe for me to pop out for a little while, dear, if I thought you seemed settled. He said he'd be calling back about now anyway, so I think I'll get going, if you don't mind. I need to collect Thistle's herbs."

I nodded, fake-smiling frantically. "No – you go. I'm great. Really happy. There's … there's a telly programme I'm just about to watch anyway. I can eat all this lunch while I watch it." The sandwich problem was solved. I'd stuff them down the side of the sofa, and text Dad before he arrived. Make him pick up some burgers.

"I'll need to leave the front door open for your dad. I'm afraid I didn't have a spare key." She twisted her fingers together, her voice even more quivery than usual. "It should be quite safe, dear. Shouldn't it?"

I wondered why she sounded so stressed out. Perhaps she thought I might try and sneak back home? The telly crackled out a glitzy game show. Gushy people winning slushy prizes. "I won't move a centimetre till Dad gets here. Promise or die." As I said it, I suddenly thought of Bibi, and the wobble-wide woman. I wondered if she'd gone back to win her prize yet. And then I remembered the narcolepsy thing, and how Bibi wasn't even real.

Barbara's mouth seemed to twist. She looked panicked.

"Are you OK?" I wondered if it should really be me looking after her, rather than the other way round

"Oh, I'm fine, dear. I felt a bit shivery all of a sudden. As if someone had just walked over my grave." She gave a small shake of her head. "I've shut the cats in the kitchen. I'll pop Mustard in there too." She puckered her ancient lips and kissed the top of the stripy cat's head. "Thistle's safe in my room. Her poorly tummy's still making her cross, so I'm keeping her away from the others. "

Mustard stared at me. I thought about Sabre.

Barbara creaked away downstairs. I grabbed my mobile from my pocket, and punched in a message.

emrgncy dbl
burger + fries
wonted

From downstairs I heard the front door open. Barbara's footsteps doddered away down the path, and headed off along Smithson Street.

My mobile bleeped.

msg recieved with
tricky client
now so rnning
late, b with u asap.

I read the message, balanced the phone on the arm of the sofa, and started squidging sandwiches down between the cushions. I squashed the biscuits down there too, scrunching them up a bit first so there'd be crumbs on the plate, and it would look like I'd really eaten them.

A car pulled up outside. Was Dad here already? He'd got those burgers a bit quick. It was more than fast food – more like food at the speed of light!

There was music coming from inside the car. Loud, boom-boom music. I heard voices too, and strained to listen. The voices were hard and loud and rough. Not Dad after all.

"Go on, do it now."

"D'you think she's in?"

"Who cares – it's not like she's gonna to do anything about it. She never does."

I heard a splat. Then another one.

"Bull's eye."

"Nice one."

"Let's do two at a time."

I clambered across the furniture and looked out of the window.

Karl Blade was in his car, the passenger door open and the engine running. Scuffer sat on the bonnet.

Both of them were yelling at Gabby, who was on the pavement.

"Go on. Chuck it harder. Try and hit the top, and then it'll ooze all the way down."

"Yo yo yo."

"Goal."

"Do it again ..."

It took only seconds for me to work out what they were hurling at the window ...

... Eggs.

Barmy Barbara
stinky house
eats raw eggs
and brain of mouse

And then Gabby pointed. I heard her say, "Think this is our lucky day. The witch has left her front door open. She must be inviting us in to eat gingerbread biscuits."

TRASHED

I thought I might make it downstairs in time to slam the door shut. Lurching across the jumbly mess, I raced onto the landing. Slid down the stairs. Stumbled at the bottom.

The door swung fully open, and in strolled Karl Blade. "Are you sure this hag won't cause us any trouble? I've seen her hobbling about but never bothered to pay her a visit before."

He stopped as he saw me. Scuffer and Gabby crowded in behind him. There was a dangerous silence.

Scuffer was the first to speak. "I seem to remember I was a little bit tied up the last time I had the pleasure of your company, and couldn't quite pay you the attention you deserved. We were looking for the witch, but this is an unexpected bonus."

Karl came very close. He stank of cigarettes. "You two know each other?"

"This is the geek that told the coppers where I lived." Scuffer narrowed his eyes. "The one who tipped them off about that burglary in those new houses. You probably don't remember, but he was with us when you picked me up that morning. The coppers gave me a bit of a description cos they were trying to catch me out, and there's not many kids round here who wear their jim-jams to school."

"Geeks annoy me. Especially those that cosy up with coppers. They're the very worst sort of geek." Karl had a soft, pinkish, piggy sort of face. "Luckily I'd already moved the goods to somewhere safe by the time the nice policeman came to see me."

I shrank backwards as far as I could, wondering whether to take a chance. Duck past him. Make a run for it. But Scuffer and Gabby were pressed right up behind him.

"And where is the old hag anyway?" Gabby leered over Karl's shoulder. "Is she bubbling up a slime-snail stew for Mad Max's dindins?"

"I don't believe the witch is here." Scuffer was bogging me out. "Otherwise she'd have been cackling round us by now."

"Lucky for us," said Gabby. "We've never had the chance to actually get inside this hovel before."

"My dad's on his way." I knew I was sounding about as threatening as a squished frog. "You'd better go or ..."

"What shall we do with him?" Scuffer's eyes gleamed, like someone about to tuck into a particularly delicious feast.

Karl took hold of my chin, moved his face close to mine, and then spat in my eye. "I think he needs a lesson."

I stayed very still. It was a struggle, but I refused to blink the gob away.

"Hit him," said Scuffer.

"Smash him up," added Gabby.

They both started making noises like mad gorillas. Ump ump ump. Uggy uggy ug.

"Mmmm. Maybe I shouldn't waste my own energy on a tadpole like this." I felt Karl loosen his hold on me. "Best I check out what's worth having upstairs. I think I'll leave the dirty end of things to you, Scuffer. Use him as a training opportunity. Part of your apprenticeship with me."

He stepped sideways, leaving just enough room to let Scuffer take his place.

"See you in five," Karl said. "It's best not to take longer than that."

I could see Scuffer's nose hairs. The stubbly bristles on his chin. The cruel sneer of his mouth.

"Perhaps you should leave us too, Sissie," he said softly. "Hear no evil. See no evil. If the nice policemen pop round our house again, better that you don't know anything about it. You sort out the front room."

"Give Bean-brain one for me," grinned Gabby. And she was gone too.

I was on my own with Scuffer.

He pressed against me, pushing. I tried to push back but he was like a sack of sand on my chest. I was trapped against the wooden banister, the stair rods pressing into my back.

Scuffer slipped his hands onto my shoulders, horribly close to my throat. Once he got started, I wouldn't stand a chance. He'd batter my baked-bean brain into a billion bits. I wouldn't be a cabbage any more. I'd be mashed potato.

"I'm gonna pulverize you, Bean-brain," he said.

What would he do first? Black my eyes? Break my nose? Smash my teeth? I was shaking. Close to throwing up. In what seemed like slow motion, his fist moved towards my face. Without planning to, or even thinking about it, I ducked.

"Aaaaaaaaaaaaaaaaaaaaaagh!" Scuffer howled.

There was the sound of wood splintering. Behind me, Barbara's banister seemed to crumple. It buckled sideways as the posts snapped. He'd missed my face, and punched right through the wood.

"My knuckle – my best fighting hand." Scuffer was the one shaking now. His eyes watered. I wasn't sure if it was because of the pain, or because he was really about to blub, but I didn't care. I wasn't going to hang around to offer him a box of tissues. Before he could try out his second best hand, I ducked past him – just as another yell roared from upstairs, mixed with a yowling miaow.

"There's a devil thing in here. Ouch. OUCH!! It's attacking me. Get it off. GET IT OFF!" Karl's voice was as shrill as a girl's. "Scuffer, get your fat backside up here. NOW!"

"I'm coming, I'm coming," Scuffer yelled back. He shot me one last look. "I'll finish this later," he growled. Then raced up the stairs.

I could hear Karl swearing on the landing. "Crazy demon thing. It's cut me."

"It's a mad cat. Gone mental from living with the witch, I should think." Scuffer sounded out of breath. "I bet you … hey, watch out! It's there, behind you. And it's gonna jump!"

But I didn't hear any more because I was out through the open front door, scrambling over the low wall that divided our houses. Had Dad put the key back after Barbara took me home the other day? I grabbed the brick, my heart thudding with the sudden fear that it might not be there. But it was. I snatched it up, fumbling for the lock. Listening for shouts. For footsteps. For the grip of a thug-hand on my shoulder.

I wouldn't make it.

They'd be out after me, more deadly than ever now.

There was a click and a rattle. The key turned. Stumbling inside the house, I slid the bolt, then raced to the dining room, dragging out chairs and stacking them against the door. They'd smash through the windows. They'd dig their way in under the floorboards. Maybe they'd come crashing down the chimney?

I was like the first pig in the fairy story Mum used to read me.

'Little pig let me in.'

'Not by the hairs on my chinny chin chin.'

Except it was Scuffer who had the hairy chin. And Karl who had the piggy pink face. Somehow the fairy story had gone all jumbled and wrong.

I sank to my knees, my hands over my ears.

There was vomit in my mouth. I spat it out. The beginnings of bruises patterned my wrists. Even with my ears covered, I could hear the blood lust next door. Uggy uggy uggy. Ump ump ump. I hoped they wouldn't make it to the kitchen. I hoped they'd leave Barbara's cats alone. It was probably already too late for Thistle.

But I couldn't go back round there to save the others. I was a wimp and a nerd and a coward. I pictured them all dead, and Barbara coming home and finding blood all over the kitchen floor. A cat massacre. Bodies scattered.

Ump ump ump. Uggy uggy uggy.

Uggy uggy uggy. Ump ump ump.

And then, all at once, the noises stopped. I heard the car start, its boom-boom music thumping as it skidded off.

I stayed where I was, thinking I should call the police. That would be the right thing to do. But I was too scared to move. And the police would definitely mean a visit from Mr Snook. I'd been left on my own *and* battered blue by the local thugs. I'd be fostered out again faster than a ferret up a trouser leg.

Tears and snot trailed down my face. I rubbed it away, still too scared to move.

Suddenly the letterbox rattled. I could see two figures through the frosted glass of the door. There were new voices. Had the police come anyway?

"He's not home. But Mum said he's being looked after by his elderly neighbour while his Dad's at work."

"Why don't we deliver all these letters round there then?"

"Because we'd have to talk to her. She's got this messed up face. Covered in scars. I know it's wrong and she can't help it, but she scares me. She scares everyone."

I knew one of the voices. I thought I probably recognised the other one too. Sophie and Jamil.

"It's OK," I called softly. "I'm here."

Fumbling and stumbling over my barricade, I clambered to let them in.

DOCUMENT OF DEATH

Barbara's kitchen door was wide open. Like a yawn. A silent shout. I wasn't ready to go out there. Not yet.

Jamil led the way into the front room, with Sophie and me following. "They've really wrecked the place." He made a clicking noise with his tongue, and shook his head.

"It's not as bad as it looks." Sophie nudged past him and straightened the lamp. The wicker basket had been emptied out, and Barbara's patchwork sewing cut to shreds. One of the cushions was slit into, then stabbed in its centre. The scissors were still jabbed inside it. Smatterings of vase lay in crystals of gold across the windowsill. The flowers were trampled into the carpet.

"Smells a bit pungent everywhere. I think they might have urinated, or defecated." Jamil sniffed the stale air, then opened the curtains.

Slimes of sticky egg were splattered across the outside of the window.

I wished he wouldn't talk in such gobbledegook. "What d'you mean?"

"He means it's smelly. Someone must have peed or pooped," said Sophie.

"Why d'you think that?"

"Intruders often behave that way," explained Jamil. "It's territorial. They're marking where they've conquered."

I wasn't quite sure what either of them was on about, but I was glad they were with me. If Miss Kindly hadn't let them deliver me a class-load of letters in the lunch break, I'd never have had the guts to go back to Barbara's on my own.

"I need to check the kitchen," I said in a hoarse voice. I hadn't warned Sophie and Jamil about the cat killings. My brain was already in overload. It was more then I could manage to explain.

I stepped cautiously back out into the hallway. "I'll come with you. Oh look … isn't she beautiful?" Sophie edged up beside me, pointing at the stairs. A huge grey cat sat glaring at us between the splintered posts. "I didn't know Barbara kept cats."

"She *had* seven." I tried to keep the wobble from my voice. "I think this one's called Thistle and I'm not keen on that growly noise she keeps making. Best not to get too close." I glanced towards the kitchen door again.

"Old ladies often have loads of cats. It's just because they're lonely."

I still hovered by the stairs, deep breathing.

Sophie frowned. I could see she was wondering what I was up to. "I'll start getting the egg off those windows. Jamil can ring school and persuade Miss Kindly we need to stay with you a bit longer – she'll trust him because he's with me – and then he can work on that front room. D'you know where the vacuum cleaner is, Max?"

I shook my head, wondering why girls always had to be so bossy. Even if I knew where the vacuum thingy was, I wouldn't know how it worked. I kept up the deep breathing. Putting off the moment of walking into that kitchen. Would we try and bury the bodies before Barbara got back? What would she want us to do?

"Come on, let's go and see what sort of a mess they've made." Sophie strode past me, obviously giving up on me and taking control. I swallowed hard and forced myself to follow.

Stepping through onto the tiled floor, we both stood together, looking round.

The kitchen was as bad as the front room.

The table had been tipped over; chairs chucked about.

"They've even emptied out the litter trays." Sophie wrinkled her nose. "How gross can you get!"

"Disgusting." But I wasn't really looking. I hardly saw any of it. I was still bracing myself for finding the bodies.

"Oh how sweet, there's another one." Sophie pointed. "Right up on top of that cupboard, there."

Looking up, I saw Blackberry blinking down. I could just about make out the other five, all huddled behind him. I felt a rush of relief. I wanted to hug them all. Except, perhaps, Thistle.

"I'll clean up the poo bits," I said, buzzed by a new burst

of energy. Clumps of stinky cat grit were nothing now.

Thistle padded in through the doorway. She sat down, tail twitching. Still glaring.

Sophie found some squeezy washing up stuff, and a bucket. She filled the bucket at the sink, and stepped over Thistle as she headed for the front door.

Thistle hissed, her ears flattened again.

I found a dustpan and brush, and swept the tiled floor. Bits of smelly cat muck stuck to the bristles, and I had to shake it out through the back door. It reminded me of George, cleaning cages. I still missed him.

"What will you tell Barbara?" Sophie came back through, sloshing eggy slime water down the sink. "She's going to be so upset."

"I'll tell her everything she wants to know. Except for the bit about them attacking me. I can pretend I was upstairs, hiding like a wimp." I hesitated. "I don't want my dad to know either." I emptied the dregs of the cat litter into the bin.

Sophie nodded and touched my arm. I liked it that she didn't ask more questions.

Jamil walked in, the shards of the vase wrapped in a patch of yellow cloth. Putting them down on the worktop, he helped me straighten the table. "I'm assuming this poor woman will want to involve the police?"

Sophie shrugged. "It's not always a good idea round here. Things like this can be hard to prove. If the ringleaders know you've blagged, it can just bring more trouble. I know, because Mum's salon gets trashed sometimes. She hardly ever reports that either."

She sloshed back outside with the bucket again.

Between us, me and Jamil pushed the table up against the wall, tucking the chairs underneath.

Jamil knelt to stroke Thistle. She fluffed her tail, then shot away down the hall, pounding back up the stairs.

"Probably not used to strangers." Jamil straightened up. "You know, it's because Barbara's different that she gets picked on. Society rejects outsiders. It's to do with the pack principle."

"You mean her scar?" Sophie was back again, tipping the next lot of sudsy water away.

"Partly. But I suspect she's eccentric. Isolated. Vulnerable." Jamil went to the worktop and played around with the crystal shards, pushing the pieces together as if it was some sort of puzzle. "This isn't as bad as it looks. I've got some awesome invisible glue back home. I might be able to fix this later."

"You'd better finish the front room before you fuss with that." Sophie put her hands on her hips. "We need to work as fast as we can."

"Yes, ma'am." Jamil saluted her, grinned at me, then headed off.

Sophie looked round the kitchen again. "Now, what else needs sorting?"

My head was suddenly throbbing and I felt vomity again. "I ... I need to sit down."

"Quick – on the chair there. Do you want water? Medicine? Are you about to pass out again?" Sophie leapt towards me. "What shall I do?"

"Nothing. It's OK" I sank onto the chair she pulled out for me. "It's just all hitting me – everything that happened."

"I'm not surprised. I'd probably be cowering in a cupboard if I'd gone through what you just have."

"I've just picked this up." Jamil appeared again, holding up shreds of buff coloured paper. "It's a Death Certificate. Dated last week."

Pulling out the chair opposite me, he sat down, ignoring Sophie's frustrated sigh. Frowning, he began sorting the scraps in the same 'jigsaw puzzle' way he'd done for the vase.

"It was her brother who died," I said. "She told me about it."

"Poor Barbara." Sophie shook her head. "What a tough time. Her brother dies. Her house gets trashed. None of us round here even knew she had any relatives. What was his name?"

Jamil slid one final puzzle piece into place and squinted. "It's an unusual one." He scanned the boxy columns, as if he was looking for some other sorts of clues. "He was called Danior. Danior Darkus. "

DESTINY

I told them everything. I had to. I apparently went so white they thought I was about to peg out. Sophie had started punching her mobile for an ambulance again.

I reminded them about that first day. Monday. Late afternoon. The time when I'd seen the fading girl. I told them about the fairground and Sabre. Bibi. Patches. Clover. Danior. And, of course, George.

"Please don't tell anyone," I begged. "You know what it's like, at school and everything."

Sophie gazed at me from across the table. "You know, that's the best thing about you. It's not that this incredible dream life has been happening - it's that you've been going through it on your own. You must have an inner strength. That's what my mum would call it. You're really special."

I didn't answer, but the way she was gazing started up my pink ear flushing.

I stared down at my hands, hoping she wouldn't notice. At school being 'special' was a kind way of saying someone had a baked-bean brain. I'd been special like that all my life.

Sophie meant a different sort of special. But there wasn't time to think through whether I believed her or not. I was battling instead to believe in George. In Patches. In all of it. "I don't get it." I looked across at Jamil. "How could it have happened?"

"I'd say you've got caught up in some sort of time loop, probably triggered by the invisible power of Barbara's feelings, which would have been heightened by the death of her brother."

I blinked at him. "A time loop?" Perhaps he was really more of a nutter than I was.

"It's not as extraordinary as you might think. The theories are based around quantum mechanics and scientists already accept that time travel is possible. The current model suggests that suitable geometries of spacetime …"

"You're saying that Max isn't dreaming at all?" Sophie cut in. "He's actually in that other time?"

Jamil looked steadily at me. I must have been gaping like a goldfish, because he took a deep breath, obviously trying to make it all bean-brain simple. "I would say Max probably enters an altered state, which opens him up to the possibility of connection with Barbara's energy field."

"So what about George?" Sophie interrupted. "How come George saw him, if the others couldn't?"

"Imagine we're all radios, and that we can 'receive' signals. One of us – probably Max - is an advanced receiver and picks up signals easily. My receivers are weaker, so I just might get moments of sound – glimpses, if you like. And

Sophie – you can't get any signal at all."

"Oh, thanks!" Sophie pulled a face, then grinned round at me. "Why do I have to be the rubbish one?"

"Purely an example. From what Max has described, George seems excessively sensitive. If he can tune in to a lion's mind-set, he might have a sensitivity for all sorts of paranormal possibilities that he's probably not even aware of."

Sophie and me looked at each other, then shrugged. "Try telling us again later. But – just for now - we want to understand what Barbara's got to do with it all." She turned back to Jamil. "How does she fit into Max's time loop thingy what's-it?"

I'd been battling that too. "There's no Barbara in my dream," I said slowly.

Jamil frowned. "I'm still certain she must be linked. The question is – why?"

He stared at me as if he thought the answer might somehow come pulsing out of my flushing pink ears. Then he pulled his iPhone from his pocket.

My brain felt like scrambled egg. I couldn't think straight.

Jamil's iPhone bleeped and flashed like an alien spaceship. "Barbara," he announced suddenly. "I've just googled the name. There's a list here. I've found a link for full names and their diminutive alternatives."

His gobbledegook rolled over me again.

And anyway, I was hardly listening. I had my own muddle of puzzles to solve. The possibilities Jamil had just hit me with made me feel vomity again. I was shaking. Sweating. Going hot, then cold. Staggering up, I lurched towards the sink.

"Bibi." Jamil spoke quietly. And then, louder, "Bibi."

I honked into the sludgy suds. "What about her?" I wiped my mouth with the back of my hand.

"Bibi is a diminutive of Barbara."

"A what?" Sophie came up behind me, rubbing my back.

"You know - a pet name - like Maddy instead of Madeline. Or Libby for Elizabeth."

I ran the tap, watching the fresh water swirl the contents of my gut away. Then I still kept watching. But it wasn't the clean spray of water I was seeing. I was picturing a little girl with long black curls and honey-gold skin.

"Did she have a scar?" Sophie's voice sounded light years away. "Max, in your time loop dream thing, did that little girl Bibi have a scar?"

The water bubbled on down the plughole. I shook my head, not sure whether to be pleased, or sorry. "No."

Sophie reached past me and turned off the tap.

I turned to face her, finding my voice at last. "So it can't be her, can it? Jamil's got it wrong."

"No, no ..." Jamil leapt up and waved his iPhone in the air, as if he'd scored a goal. "This is the missing link. The final piece of the puzzle."

Dimly, from the front of the house, I heard the door open.

"This is why you've been tapped into Barbara and Bibi. They're the same person and *you* are a scientific breakthrough. Awesome! If you're experiencing that dream in a time before her accident happened - whatever it was – you'll have the power to prevent its occurrence. Just think what that means."

"What does it mean?" Sophie glanced at me. I had turned to face Jamil.

"If Max can gain control of the sequence of events that play out in his dream-state, he can reshape Barbara's destiny."

Sophie pressed her knuckles against her lips. Her eyes glistened and she was doing the gazing again. "You can give Barbara the gift of a different life." Her voice was all gushy and excited. "We won't tell her because she'd never believe us, but if you could only ..."

"My oh my." The quivery voice in the doorway made us all jump as if we'd been caught with our hands in the biscuit jar. "Max? Hasn't your dad come yet? Is everything all right?

CURSED

I decided that bossiness in girls was a good thing after all.

Sophie took charge. She made Barbara her favourite herb tea. She sat her down in the front room. She explained about the trashing. Jamil showed her the broken vase and jabbered on about technological breakthroughs with glue.

"So what do you want to do?" Sophie perched on the arm of Barbara's chair. "We can contact the police and Max can give a statement?"

"There's bound to be fingerprints. Scrapings of skin. All manner of forensic evidence," Jamil added.

Me and Jamil sat cross-legged on the floor by the window. There were three cats on the other chair. Two more at Barbara's feet. Mustard was draped round her neck again, and Thistle crouched on her lap, still glaring.

Barbara sipped her tea, her hand shaking. "I've had the police in before, and the trouble stops for a while. But it always comes back in the end."

"We'll do our best to raise awareness round here, I promise you that." Jamil nodded towards her. "I could set up some sort of online 'good neighbour' campaign. Minority groups can make a difference."

"I've learnt to live with it." Barbara glanced nervously at me and Jamil. "The same as I learnt to live with the scar."

And then Sophie said it. She asked the question straight out. Not pink eared. Not awkward. She asked it as easily as if she was asking where Barbara bought her shoes. "So how did you get that scar? What actually happened?"

Barbara sipped her tea again. I felt as if weeks were passing. Months. Years.

"My family were travellers," she said at last. Her voice seemed very faint. As if she was talking from far away.

I saw Sophie squeeze her frail shoulder.

Barbara breathed out slowly. "My dad trained big cats for the circus. Lions mostly. But as the war dragged on, no one had any money to come to the shows. Not enough to keep us all fed. So Da got Danior take over the act, and joined the army. There was lots of bad things happening to gypsies in Europe. Terrible things. I've learnt about it since … Ma always said my dad was a special sort of person. Extra kind. Do anything for anyone. She said Da had wanted to do what he could to fight against all the cruelty … "

"Go on." Sophie smiled the smile of an angel.

"I've never explained all this to anyone before, dear. I never even knew my Dad, you see. I wasn't born when he went to the war. I just used to sit with Ma outside the trailer at night, and she'd tell me lots of stories about him. I think really she was telling them to herself though. I think it was the way she could keep him with her."

"My mum says it's good to talk. Even about sad things."

Barbara nodded, finishing the last of her tea. "Ma said my dad believed the fighting would stop soon anyway, and he'd have a soldier's pay in his pocket to bring to us. Except the war finished, so my dad had been right about that, but he never came back. Missing presumed dead – that was what the army told Ma. Danior took it badly. He tried to be strong for Ma, but something in his head got tainted with wicked thoughts. Or maybe it was his heart that got twisted." She sighed and rattled her cup down into the saucer. "Danior's passed on now, though. Just last week."

"You've finished your tea," said Sophie softly. "Let me take that from you." She put the empty cup and saucer on the carpet.

Barbara kept talking. "Poor Danior asked to see me before he died, but I couldn't go to him. I convinced myself I couldn't leave the cats, but I'm afraid I was probably just being a stubborn old woman. Still upset that he and Ma never came to see me. I was so very lonely, growing up, dear."

"It's all so sad." Sophie's eyes were glistening. "Why d'you think they did that?"

"The circus couldn't risk me being around any more. They'd be afraid I'd bring more bad luck. I was tainted. Cursed. And besides, Ma couldn't have looked after me. Not with all the travelling – I needed lots of operations. One of her skills was to make the costumes for the performers, but she couldn't have stitched me together again." Barbara plucked at her cardigan, then rubbed the backs of her hands. "I did learn to sew like my ma though. The nurses used to whip me because of my traveller ways. They made me call myself Barbara. They said it would be better to forget everything to do with my family, so sewing became my special secret. It helped me feel closer to Ma." She shook her head. "I've done a lot of sewing over the years."

We all sat in silence. I felt dizzy again, and hoped I wasn't going to have another burst of honking.

"How long were you in hospital for?" Sophie asked gently.

"A long, long time, dear. The council didn't move me here until I was all grown up. I wasn't in a normal hospital, you see …" Barbara's one eye peered out at us, as if she thought we might get up and run for it. Her voice faltered, "… I was in an asylum. A madhouse. I wasn't mad, but they didn't know what else to do with me. I remember I cried a lot." Her shaking twig fingers stroked Thistle's head, faster and faster. It must have hurt, but for the first time she looked almost happy. Almost like she might start purring. "The nurses used to lock me in a padded cell because I disturbed the other patients. I probably did end up silly in the head, because of that."

"It sounds like a nightmare."

"They even took my voice away from me. They used to shout and say I spoke all wrong. One nurse beat me and beat me, until I sounded out my words the way she wanted."

"You must have had some sort of inner strength." Sophie

glanced at me, then turned her attention back to Barbara again. "After all, you've survived. You're here today, telling us about it."

"I wish I could believe that, dear." Barbara began rocking slightly, her hands crossed over her chest. She shook her head and sighed deeply, as if she was coming up for air. "The asylum looked out over the woods. You know, the ones up by the park?"

I was staring at her. My gut turned and churned with this new piece of horror. George had said the madhouses were cruel places. Wicked. Everything about Barbara's life just got worse and worse and worse.

"You probably know the asylum as a crumbling, broken building. Once they closed it down it stayed empty for years. The woods were a comfort through all the time I lived there, though. Just looking out of the tower windows brought back happier memories." She looked round at us all. "I'd been running free in them you see, the day it all happened. Playing with my new puppy, and picking flowers for Ma."

Sophie glanced at me, and then at Jamil.

Jamil nodded, as if everything he'd said was making sense. Like an invisible puzzle coming together.

Which it sort of was.

"So, your scar," Sophie said, reaching for Barbara's hand. "You still haven't said exactly how you got it."

Long minutes ticked by. I thought maybe Sophie had gone too far. Maybe this was one question too many. But then Barbara rasped out another long breath. "The guv'nor of the small circus we were in took on a cage boy. George. It was his job to look after the big cats. Clean the cages and such. I liked George. I suppose I loved him, in my little girl way."

I had to stop myself jumping up and yelling. I was bubbling up with feelings. Half laughing. Half crying. I pressed my knuckles against my mouth to stop everything from spilling out.

"Danior and George didn't get on, though. George was a runaway. It wasn't so unusual then. Fairgrounds and circuses drew in a lot of those wandering souls in the years after the war."

I wanted to join in. To ask questions. To add things. I realised I was biting my knuckles. Drawing blood.

"The boys fell out over a particular big cat that the guv'nor was pinning his hopes on. George was angry about the way the cat was being trained. Danior didn't have a special way with the cats, not like my dad had done. And George *did* have that special way. That, I suppose, is why it happened."

She stared at her twig wrinkled hands.

"Why? What happened?" Sophie spoke gently, her voice ghost faint.

"George was a josser. Not a true circus traveller. Everyone said you couldn't trust jossers, but I'd trusted him." Barbara's voice grew even fainter than Sophie's. "But I shouldn't have done. I was too young to really know about the good and bad in people. Especially jossers."

"Go on." I wriggled up onto my knees.

"It was night time. Just before midnight. The funfair that the guv'nor had got to tour with us was still open. Once it stopped, we'd have all got packed up ready to move on to the next village." Her voice drifted and it was hard to hear her clearly.

My heart was bashing out a circus drumroll.

"I'd gone round to the wagon where the cat was kept, because I'd left my little chimp's jacket behind. She wasn't too well and she felt the cold a lot. My new puppy was with me too. I'd really taken to him, and I remember cuddling him that evening. Whispering that I'd always keep him safe." Barbara took another wheezing breath. "George let the cat out. It attacked me. It tore half of my face off."

I almost fell forward onto the carpet. "George let the lion out?" I wanted to argue. He wouldn't. He wouldn't. And then I remembered something I'd said, at the time when Danior locked George in the cage. *Don't you ever want to set him free? Give him the chance to just run for his life?*

Was it me who'd put that thought in his head? I forced myself to stay quiet and keep listening.

Barbara's voice drifted again. "I never understood why he did it. George might have been a josser, but he knew about animals. He'd have known all the dangers. But I've had years to think about it – years and years." She shook her head. "It must have been spite. Jealousy. He was jealous that Danior had an act, and he must've known that he'd never get the chance. The guv'nor wouldn't have risked a josser in the ring."

Sophie glanced at me, then looked back at Barbara again.

I wondered if I looked as ghostly white as I felt.

"So this josser George?" I said faintly. "What happened to him?"

"He disappeared. The police came to the asylum to tell me they were looking for him. They said he was criminally responsible. I don't believe they ever found him."

"What do you think about him now?" I almost whispered the question.

Barbara hunched forward. "The priest at the asylum said we should forgive the sins of others, but I lost everything that night. My family. My way of life. And my future. I'm getting on in years now, and no doubt I'll be following Danior soon enough. I sometimes wonder if I should try and forgive George before that happens. But it's so very difficult for me." She shook her head. "That wicked twist that happened in Danior's heart – I'm afraid to say it's probably happened in mine too."

We sat without speaking, only Thistle's purrs thrumming the silence.

There was a rattle on the window. "Barbara? Max? Can you let me in?"

It was Dad.

Jamil got up. I heard them talking before they came through. "Traffic's been terrible, and then there were queues at McDonald's. I've been trying to ring Max but he hasn't been answering. But it looks like he's having a good time. Like he's had some company."

Dad burst in to where we were all sitting, and I could see from his face-splitting smile that he thought it was brilliant that I'd got visitors.

"Max, mate – sorry I've been so long. I've got the burgers but they might be a bit cold. I don't suppose you've got a microwave, Barbara?"

I squeezed my eyes shut, terrified I might blub in front of everyone.

All I could think was that Bibi's horrible future was my fault.

MEDDY-TASTING

It was Saturday afternoon. Getting late. Dad had given me an hour at the park – the first time I'd been allowed out since I'd been in hospital. 'Don't go anywhere else. Just stay with your friends. Keep your mobile switched on, and be back before *it gets dark.'*

We walked down Smithson Street, Sophie and Jamil either side of me. It had been a warm day, and everywhere was busy with people washing cars, trimming hedges, watering plants. Ordinary things.

"I was up early this morning, researching probabilities." I could tell Jamil was struggling to put whatever it was he'd researched into 'bean-brain' language. "What we need to do is get you back into that time, get you so George doesn't let Sabre free. Get you in a position to be able to stop it all from ever happening."

"I've told you before, it's not that easy."

A little girl was sitting in her front garden, making a daisy chain while her dad piled up weeds into a wheelbarrow. I felt my gut twist. Ordinary things. Nothing would ever feel 'ordinary' again. "I can't just slip back when I feel like it. And even if I could, things just happen around me. I don't have any control. I can't even touch anything."

"You're in a form of dream state," Jamil agreed. "I haven't quite worked out a way to empower you. Give you some actual impact."

"I've got an idea." Sophie nudged me suddenly, stepping ahead and walking backwards a few paces as if her plan would make more sense to me if I could see her face. "Remember that lucid dreaming I told you about? That day I told you about my undies dream."

My ears flushed pink. Would they always do that every time a girl said the word 'undies'?

If Sophie noticed, she didn't say. "You just decide to stay awake, even though you're dreaming, and then you can take charge of things. Change the endings."

"I still have to get there." I managed to sound casual again.

"That's easier," said Jamil. "We just find the exact spot that took you there the first time. It'll be somewhere that matters to Barbara. Somewhere she keeps going back to. Her moods and memories will be trapped there."

"D'you think those flowers are important too?" I asked. "My dream-time place always reeks of them."

"More than likely. Or at least, not the flowers themselves – just the smell. Our nostrils contain cells that store memories. In the same way that we remember things that we see, these cells remember specific scents – and once a smell triggers these memory cells, our subconscious mind can slip us back to the place where it was first significant. So the flower scents are evoking a happier time for Barbara, and Max is tapping into a channel of energy that's linking back to that time."

"Do you really know everything about *everything*?" Sophie sighed, and nudged me.

"We knows what our noses knows," I said, nudging her back. "Get it?"

"Oh, genius, Max. I'd forgotten about your silly sense of humour." Sophie sighed again, but she grinned at me too, so I knew I hadn't really annoyed her.

We reached the edge of the park.

There was a woman with a fluffy grey dog on the far side, and a couple of boys playing football. "I'll give it a go," I said uncertainly. "But I'm not sure it'll work."

"You need to believe in it. Positive thinking. That's what my mum says." Sophie was still locking eyes with me.

"We have to go to the edge of the wood, then. That's where I first saw Bibi." I walked round Sophie and went on ahead. The branches still towered, but nothing felt spooky this time. I couldn't catch the sense of anything weird. I turned as the others walked up behind me. "This is it. I remember this knobbled old tree."

Jamil leant forward, running his finger across the words dug into the bark. "I wonder who wrote this?"

"Probably an asylum patient," said Sophie softly. "We know how grim it was."

We stood in silence. I was thinking about padded cells and stiff-faced nurses, and a lonely little girl gazing sadly out through a tower window.

From somewhere deep amongst the trees, a pigeon hooted. The sound was soft. Magical. Sophie and Jamil looked at me, as if I was the one with all the answers. "Don't," I said. "Don't stare at me like that."

Sophie gave a nervous giggle. "Sorry, to be honest I'm a bit scared. I don't really know what to expect."

"I don't know either, but just promise not to panic or ring ambulances, however weird I look."

"We promise. I mean, you always come out of it in the end, don't you? You looked a bit dazed that time when I found you, but you never get hurt or anything. How can you - you're a sort of ghost."

"A ghost from the future. An awesome phenomenon." Jamil punched the air with his fist. "If you can get control of this, just think what the possibilities might be for all humanity."

I didn't really care about all humanity. All I wanted was to make things all right for Barbara.

We stood around. The sky turned dusk grey. Streaks of blood-red tainted the wispy clouds.

"Maybe we should sit down?" Sophie sounded anxious again. "I'm a bit worried about Max falling over if he suddenly 'goes' there."

We sat. The pigeon was still calling; over and over again.

I wished and wished and wished myself back into my dream world, scrunching my eyes and clenching my fists, trying to soak in Barbara's invisible time loop energy.

The ground was lumpy. Uncomfortable. I could hear Sophie breathing.

And suddenly, Jamil laughed. He let out a great snorting hoot. As if he'd pressed some sort of invisible button, Sophie joined in. She shrieked and giggled and rolled over, clutching her side. I felt my ears flush pink. Burning. They were making a joke out of me. This whole thing had been some ugly, terrible game.

"Oh sorry, Max." Sophie had her hand clapped across her mouth. "It just feels so … so …"

And looking at her face, her eyes bright and friendly, I knew it wasn't bad laughing. It was more the naughty laugh-feeling I got at school sometimes, like the day when our Headmistress did a fart and we all had to pretend not to notice. And I joined in, my own laugh fizzing up like bubbles in a bottle. I let myself slip sideways and collapsed on Sophie. All three of us writhed and kicked and spluttered. When we finally stopped and lay on our backs, looking up at the darkening sky, Jamil said, "It's not going to work."

I felt flattened out then. A failure. Suddenly it wasn't funny any more.

"I've got another idea." Sophie sat up and hugged her knees. "My mum meditates. She has friends round and they sit in a circle with a candle burning, and they make themselves focus. Why don't we try something like that?"

I was still feeling hopeless. "Sounds a bit spooky."

Sophie screwed up her face. "How can you, of all people, be worried about that?"

"And what if Scuffer turns up? Or even Gabby?" None of us had mentioned them up until now, but they'd been shadows in my thoughts. A distant danger. And the darker it got, the more chance that they'd come looking for trouble.

Jamil straightened up, brushing dead leaves from his jeans. "The most they can do is beat us up, nick our mobiles and leave us for dead."

Sophie nudged him. "So not much to worry about then."

I wriggled over so I was facing them both. I wasn't going to let Scuffer or Gabby mess anything up for Barbara again. I was going to do this. I was going to make it work. "Right," I said, "this meddy tasting stuff your mum does. Let's try it."

"Meditation." Sophie bent and picked another leaf from the ground. "You need to have something to focus on. Look at this, and concentrate. Mum says it helps shut out the clutter of everyday life."

She stuck the leaf on the grass in front of us, then took hold of my hand and squeezed it softly. It felt weird holding hands. I couldn't even remember the last time I'd done it. Only with Mum. In hospital. Her last few days.

"You ready?" Sophie dropped her voice to a churchy

quiet, and let go of my hand.

"Yep. Think so," I murmured back. I fixed my gaze on the leaf.

It was pale green mixed with lemon yellows and the edges were zaggedy. Tiny hairs dusted across it like soft fur. So many patterns. So many colours. I'd never looked at a leaf properly before.

"Now, Max," Sophie's voice was still gentle, "this is just about you – you have to keep concentrating. And when you're ready, you need to bring up a picture in your mind. Probably George's face, or Sabre or something. Keep thinking about them over and over again."

"Choose Sabre." Jamil's voice had dropped too, as if any sudden sound might snap the spell we were all desperate to weave. "Or maybe even just his blue eyes. You'll need a powerful but simple image to work with. What happens next, Soph?"

"Once you've got the picture in your mind, you hold it steady. And then make it grow stronger in your imagination. Make those lion eyes get brighter. Dazzling bright. So bright, they could burn. And just keep watching them over and over again."

I stared at the leaf until my eyes stung. An ant marched a ragged path across it. "Hello, Mr Ant," I said softly.

"Shhh," whispered Sophie.

"Keep concentrating," murmured Jamil. "You need your mental energies directed into the thought process. The neural pathways will carry signals along the sensors to ensure a state of deep relaxation."

The ant scuttered along the edge of the leaf and dropped down into the grass. I wasn't managing to picture Sabre's eyes.

Directing mental energies was a tough thing to get right.

The tip of the leaf curled backwards slightly. The curled-back tip was a soft brown. I thought about leaves decaying. Going brittle. Crunched into dust. I still couldn't see Sabre's eyes.

One of the football playing boys shouted something about a rubbish goal.

His voice sounded strange and hollow and distant.

I heard snuffling. Something was sniffing my shoulder. Was I halfway back into all those years ago? I wanted to look round, but if the meddy tasting was working at last, I didn't want to risk taking my eyes off that leaf. But maybe the 'something' sniffing my shoulder was Sabre? Was the escaped Sabre going to munch me up instead of Bibi? What possibilities for the future of humanity would come out of that?

"Come, Rexie; here, Rexie. Come on, sorry – oh no, really sorry ..."

Footsteps thudded towards us. I tore my gaze away from the leaf, just in time to see the fluffy grey dog about to cock its leg on Jamil's shoulder.

"Oh, gross!" Sophie sprang up.

Jamil flapped his arm. "I don't think it *quite* got me."

"Sorry." The owner grabbed the dog's collar. "Naughty boy. No!" She gave Jamil a weak smile. "Sorry. You were, well, just in the way. He always goes on that particular bit of grass. I don't know why."

"It's territorial." Jamil got to his feet. "It's what canines do."

"Terrier torial," I said, even though I'd lost the mood for jokes.

Rexie was dragged away to be territorial somewhere else.

I stood up beside Jamil.

Sophie looked at me. "Did you get anything? Was it starting to happen?"

I shook my head, my voice flat and sorry. "Too many noises."

"The brain has the power to block out irrelevant sound if – "

"Not now, Jamil." Sophie wrinkled her nose. "D'you want to try again? Now you've got the hang of it? I could do it with you, while Jamil stands guard against tiddling terriers. It might help to chant. I think my mum does that, now I come to think about it. We could repeat something like 'Sabre's blue eyes, Sabre's blue eyes' over and over and over."

"Keep your eyes shut tight, to prevent unwanted visual stimulus sending data to your brain." Jamil gave Sophie a sideways glance, as if he was waiting for her to stop him again, and then rattled on. "It's like a computer going into hibernation."

I closed my eyes, hearing the sound of a motorbike thrumming from somewhere near the flats. A helicopter hummed overhead, and I wondered if it was going off to land on the flat roof of the hospital. I started imagining a spider had dropped down from one of the branches and was crawling down inside my t-shirt. I could actually feel it. I knew it wasn't there really … but … I opened my eyes, and smacked at my back and my shoulders.

"What's up? What's happening?" Sophie was jumping to her feet, eyes wide with alarm.

"I can't do it. I can't think for long lumps of time. Even Miss Kindly says I'm rubbish at all that concentration stuff." I snatched the leaf up, ripped it in half, then chucked it back into the grass. It was useless. I was useless. The saving Barbara moment was like a lifetime away. And even if I *had* been able to concentrate, could I really get back there just by staring at a crummy leaf, and picturing Sabre's eyes? "I don't believe in all this meddy tasting. It's stupid." And just in that second my mobile beeped. A message from Dad.

I made myself calm down, holding the screen up for them to read:

time u wur bck!

"I'm sorry. I know you've both been trying to help. I'm just rubbish at lots of things. And now I've got to go. My dad's under doctor's orders for my meal times and bed times and stuff. He'll come looking for me if I don't head

185

off now. It was hard enough getting out in the first place."

We walked away from the park. Away from my dream. Away from my one chance to change Bibi's future.

SHADOWY SHAPE

I couldn't sleep. My duvet was too hot. I pushed it away. I got cold. I pulled it back over me.

My mobile screen showed:

22:47

Nearly eleven o'clock.

Barbara said Sabre got her just before midnight. I shivered, even though I was too hot again. Years and years ago, something terrible was about to happen at the end of my road.

I got out of bed and shuffled to the window.

From downstairs I could hear the click of the computer keyboard. Dad was working out his window-selling maths money.

I squinted out at the moonlit sky, feeling hopeless and helpless.

After the failed meddy tasting, Sophie and Jamil had come in for a while.

Dad did us pizzas, and Jamil rattled on about his Quantum Mechanics thing while we ate them. It was all discovered by some bloke called Einstein. According to Einstein, time could loop back on itself. Jamil insisted that was what I was doing in my dream. Looping back. I was connecting with Bibi's world because Barbara, in her memories, was still living there herself. He'd tried several ways to explain it, and it still kept scrambling my brain, but I couldn't really argue with him. I couldn't come up with anything better.

The night stretched forever.

A car exhaust backfired, exploding like a gun.

A shadowy shape moved in the garden. Something was squeezing through a gap in the fence that ran between our house and Barbara's. I drew a panicked breath and stepped backwards, thinking it might be Scuffer. He could shin up the drainpipe and smash his way in through my bedroom window. He'd finish what he started.

But it wasn't Scuffer. It was a fox. It stared towards our house for a moment, its eyes glowing gold in the moonlight. Then, slinking, it turned and headed towards the back-gate bins. There'd be rubbish all over the alley by morning.

I wondered what Barbara would have been like if Sabre hadn't got her?

Maybe she'd have married a clown? She might have had children. She'd be a granny by now.

And what about George? Barbara had said the guv'nor would never give a josser an act, but he might have risked it, if he'd seen Sabre eat from George's hand like a kitten.

George had been good to me, in the past. Barbara had tried to look after me in the present. I was letting them both down. I went back to my bed and sat huddled on the edge. My mobile glowed out:

22.55

And then I thought - if Dad was sorting out his earnings, he'd be busy for hours.

I could sneak out the back, and follow the fox past the bins. It didn't even matter if I got caught. I'd say I was sleep walking, and Dad would write it down in the sleep diary.

I crept down the stairs, my heart jumping at every creak. Moving in silent slow-motion, I edged my bare feet into my trainers, then slunk, fox-like, along the hall to the kitchen. The back door wasn't locked. I opened it slowly. Slowly. Closing it behind me.

And then I was free, hurrying towards the back gate. Knocking the bins as I squeezed past; my trainers scrunched on an empty box of Choco Krispies. I edged into the alley, glimpsing the fox loping ahead of me, melting into the darkness.

I took a deep breath. I knew I was going to look pretty stupid, running down the road in my Spidermans again, but there hadn't been time to flaff about getting dressed.

I was going to have one last try at getting back to my dream, and there was only one place to do it.

SHIVERING SILENCE

The park was quiet. I sat by the knobbly tree again.

ENTER IF YOU DARE

The damp grass seeped through my Spiderman bottoms. I hoped Scuffer Dobbs wasn't lurking in the shadows. He'd say I'd wet the bed. He'd say that just before he smacked me in the mouth, of course.

At least there were no dogs being terrier torial.

As far as I could tell, there was no one in the park at all.

I wondered suddenly if George had died. He'd be older than Barbara.

The moon hung like a huge silver penny. The branches of the trees scratched crazy patterns against the night. A wind sprang up and shivered the leaves. Shivering me.

I wished I'd remembered my dressing gown.

Looking all around, I tried to picture the park of my dream. I thought about where Sabre's wagon was. Where the rides were. The Big Top. But the details were hazy.

My mind wasn't hazy though. I was buzzing with a sort of locked-up energy. I stared at the moon, and tried to see Sabre's eyes staring back, blue-fire magic against the silver. The lion in the moon. I kept whispering the words over and over, *the lion in the moon, the lion in the moon.*

It wasn't working.

My eyes started watering. The moon went blurry, like a smudge. As if it was being washed away. My eyes stung from all the staring so I closed them, pressing against them with my knuckles. I could still see the smudged moon on the inside of my lids.

I kept my eyes pressed shut. I needed to fall asleep. That was how I'd got there before. *Let me sleep let me sleep.* My brain was still buzzing. I'd never felt so wide awake.

Mum used to make me count sheep if I couldn't sleep.

I couldn't always remember Mum, but I missed everything about her.

"One – two – three …" The sheep pushed and jostled. They bleated, trotting down a farm track, a boy with wild-mane hair walking behind them. "Seventeen- eighteen – nineteen …" I heard someone whistling, but it wasn't quite a whistle. The sound seemed to come from above the wind. The sheep came closer. Right up to me. Their bodies were soft clouds. And Max smelt something. Peachy. Sweet. And he was falling through peach-sweet softness.

"Ninety-nine, a hundred, a hundred and ..."

And then came the scream ...

DEAD LOCKED

It was a terrible screeching. A long scratch of fear.

Max jumped to his feet, thinking his heart was going to explode out of his chest ... and he saw Clover, crouching outside the tent, chattering to herself.

It was only noisy chimp-chat.

She wasn't wearing the red jacket, and he'd forgotten how manky her fur was without it.

It was night, but not the same night as he'd just left. This night had no moon. Just a billion, pinprick stars in the blue-velvet sky.

There were lights everywhere, torches and lanterns all hung from poles. Their flickering made everything magical. Colours glittered and sparked like Christmas baubles.

Max could make out Bibi, kneeling in a shadowed gap between the trailers. She kept giggling, murmuring to Patches as she arranged a crown of yellow flowers on his head. George came whistling out of the tent, pushing a wheelbarrow piled high with stinky sawdust.

Max tried to whistle back, but whistling was another

thing he'd never managed to master. "Wow - it worked. I'm here."

George grinned as he walked over to him. "Wow indeed," he said. He put the barrow down.

Max looked across to where the funfair sparkled; music pulsing across the night. "I've never seen it lit at night before. The colours are magical." He hesitated, searching for the right word. "Bedazzling."

"It's been a promising day. Busy. The guv'nor's been dancing round the rides, whirling his hat about and telling everyone they're wonderful!" George winked and checked over his shoulder before lowering his voice. "I'm going to try and make good use of his mood. I'm going to tell him about my act."

"Sounds great." It didn't sound great at all really. It sounded as if time was running out. Max needed to come up with an idea straight away.

Jamil had explained that Max had to find a way to stop things happening, but he mustn't talk about what he knew. Talking might end up with George thinking he was mad, and then he wouldn't do whatever Max wanted him to do.

"How's Sabre?" Max said cautiously.

"Fine. I stayed here all afternoon, making doubly sure Danior didn't turn up with his dentist chum again. We move on in the morning, so he'll be safe once we're at West Hollow. For a while, at least. I just need to buy some time … long enough for the guv'nor to see what I'm capable of."

"Is Danior still letting you in Sabre's cage? You've still got the key and everything?"

"He'd replace me like a shot if he got the chance, but cage boys like me can be almost as hard to find as tamers. Danior wouldn't want to get his own hands dirty."

"Where is Danior anyway?" Max realised it wasn't just the night that was clear. His mind was clear too. Thinking straight, blade sharp. He must be having a lucid dream. It was all working out right.

"Danior's got lucky with a girl. He's gone off somewhere with her. He won't be back for a while."

"Is Sabre's cage door locked? Is it *definitely* locked?" Max wondered if he was giving too much away, but it was important to know if the unlocking had already happened.

"Of course it's locked. What kind of a duffer d'you think I am?"

George glanced towards Bibi. "Come here, sweetheart, have some fun before the stalls start packing up again. Get yourself some candyfloss." He reached in his pocket and flipped a silver coin as she came skipping towards him. Patches bounded with her, yapping and wagging his tail. Clover chattered happily when she saw them.

"Danior said I has to stay near to Sabre." The lights flickered round Bibi like busy fairies. She was wearing a yellow dress; a scar of black stitches zigzagging up one edge of the skirt. She looked so young, and so small. Max wondered if, when he changed the future, her grandchildren would look like her. He *had* to get this right.

"Don't worry. Danior won't be back tonight. I need to

have a chat to the guv'nor, but he'll be doing his after-show walkround, so he'll be coming this way soon. I'll stay close enough to keep an eye on the cat. Trust me."

Bibi hesitated.

Max remembered that smack on the face.

"Go on. Enjoy what's left of the night. It'll be all work again tomorrow."

"Promise Danior isn't goin' to know, Georgie?"

"I promise, sweetheart. Go on – quickly – before I attack you and tickle you to death …" George gave a lion type growl and twisted his hands into claws.

Bibi shrieked, giggled, and skipped away. Clover and Patches kept up either side of her.

George steered the wheelbarrow between the nearby trailers. Max kept close to him. He wasn't going to let him out of his sight. They passed Natty, and she shifted restlessly. George stopped and stroked the bear's scrubby coat. She closed her eyes and grunted with pleasure.

Rounding the back of the trailers, George emptied the smelly waste into a heap. The stink leaked out, even worse than before.

"Yuck." Max pulled a face.

"Don't worry. I'll rake it down before we leave. We don't want any complaints from the locals. There's top quality manure mixed up in there, though. They could grow prize-winning cabbages in it."

They headed back to the tent, and George's mood seemed to change. Max felt he could sense something. Nerves?

Tension? Had the idea of letting Sabre out struck him already? He couldn't see why. Not if George wanted to show the guv'nor his act.

And then George put the barrow down, and looked at Max steadily. "I don't think I'll see you again."

"What?" Max wondered, for a moment, if George knew what was going to happen. Wondered if he knew that tonight he would do something so terrible, he'd have to run away and never see *any* of them again. But that was crazy – George would never have done it if he could have seen Bibi's terrible future.

"Your spirit belongs here. You won't be able to follow me tomorrow. And … I want to tell you …" George sounded awkward, "you've been pretty good company, for a ghost."

Max felt his ears flush up. "And you. I mean, you've been pretty good company as well."

They grinned at each other, and somehow in those grins all the things they hadn't said got understood.

They sat together, waiting for the guv'nor, and Max felt a mix of sad and happy feelings muddling through him. Sad because this was the end of knowing George. Happy because, if he got it right tonight, he'd have done what the future wanted him to do.

And suddenly, a fresh thought cracked through him. When George explained about his act, the guv'nor was going to turn him down. Max could feel it in his invisible bones. Barbara had even said it. He'd 'never let a josser in the ring'. If the guv'nor had turned George down, that would explain why he'd done what he did. A stab of hopeless frustration. A rare rush of anger. Max knew what all those things felt like.

And so all Max had to do was to stop George from talking to the guv'nor. If George didn't talk to the guv'nor before midnight, the anger thing wouldn't happen. He wouldn't let Sabre out. And Bibi would never get hurt.

But what could he do? Even with his lucid dreaming, he wasn't sure he could stop the guv'nor from appearing round that corner. "What time is it?"

George glanced up at the stars, and then back at Max. "Just after half eleven, I'd say. Why?"

Max's gut gave a panicked twist. He had less than half an hour.

And suddenly he was gripped by another moment of brilliance, an idea more dazzling than anything he'd ever had before. He knew the perfect way to keep George from talking to the guv'nor before midnight. It might mean Bibi got into trouble for leaving Sabre again. Danior might give her another smack. But George had said that Danior wasn't around, and the risk he might come back was better than the alternative. A zillion times better.

Max swallowed hard. He wasn't going to enjoy it, but it was the only thing that would definitely work. "If you don't think we'll ever see each other again, we should do something special tonight."

George raised one eyebrow. "What did you have in mind?"

A sick feeling began to wind through Max's gut. "Take me on the roller coaster."

Both George's eyebrows shot up. "That's a mad idea. Last time you tried something scary, you disappeared again. I don't think you'd be able to do it."

"I won't be scared this time. I've been learning special mind-control stuff. It's called meddy tasting. I can think myself into feeling OK about things."

"Sounds like there's time to kill out in that limbo of eternity you must float about in." George shook his head, then grinned. "Time to kill. Sorry. Not a good use of words. But anyway, back to the roller ride idea – I don't mind that you can't manage things like that. I'm happy for us just to sit here. You can tell me everything about life when you were alive. It'll make it easier for me to trace who you were. What era you lived in."

"If I don't do it now, and I never see you again, I might spend forever kicking myself for being such a coward. And if I manage to do that mind control thing, I might be able to follow you to West Hollow. Maybe even further. Invisible friends can have all sorts of uses."

Max could see George thinking it through. Thinking how amazing it might be.

George glanced towards the tent. "I'm supposed to …"

"Please." It was blackmail, but Max had no choice.

George looked at Max and his eyes were sad. "I do want to make this last night as special as possible, but I've told Bibi …"

"Please."

George looked all round, checking between the shadowy

trailers and scanning the park for as far as he could see. "If Danior *does* come back ..."

"Extra massively big please."

Suddenly George grinned. "You win. I wouldn't want to leave your soul tortured for all of eternity. But we'd better get ourselves over there now. There might be a queue, and it's nearly midnight. The rides will be stopping soon."

Max wanted to leap about, punching the air in victory. He was going to do it. It didn't matter how scared he might be - he was inside the moment when he changed the future.

ROLLER RIDE

The passengers screamed. Max stood beside George in the queue for the next ride, and tried not to listen. The train hurtled. It slowed. It tilted sideways, rattling and whooshing round a bend. It slowed again. At the very top, just before the big drop, it hovered.

Max blinked up at it; the engine was actually pushing off the track, jutting in mid air.

The screams were like a thousand nightmares.

Max wondered whether if he focused on Dad's face, he would wake up? He could be home and in bed in five minutes, tucked safely under his quilt.

He made himself think about Barbara's scar instead. He made himself think about Bibi.

The engine lurched. It was moving again, gathering speed, screeching down the switchback drop. Max saw it tilt as it raced round the corner, and then roll back to the beginning.

It chugged innocently past the point where Max and George were waiting, and stopped. Everyone clambered out. They all looked pale-faced and shaky, but they were laughing. Some rejoined the queue behind Max and George.

"You're still sure?" George murmured from the corner of his mouth.

Max made himself think into the faraway future. "I'm still sure."

The carriage was black. The seats were slime-green. Max was relieved that at least they weren't sitting at the front. George shoved himself up against the far side. "I normally sit in the middle when I'm on my own, but it's best you have your own space. Otherwise you might end up on my lap."

"Won't we be unbalanced?" Max thought how being unbalanced might make the carriage tip. There were a zillion ways for his dreaming self to fall. If he fell, he might wake up again. He'd have to concentrate. Meddy taste.

The safety bar that Max couldn't hold was decorated with skulls.

He sat hunched forward with his hands in his lap.

Other people clambered on, in front and behind.

George whistled as Loo-brush shuffled by, collecting money for the ride. He was dressed in the baggy star-patterned trousers and braces again. "I like your outfit. You look impressive."

"Thanks, Bibi's mum helped with the finishing touches." Loo-brush's mouth was painted with a red sausage smear of lipstick. He smiled his miserable smile, and his tombstone teeth glowed a dull yellow against the powdery white of his face. "You all done for the night, George?"

"Pretty well." George nodded. "The cats are settled. There's nothing much to do till we start dismantling everything. Have you seen the guv'nor about?"

"There was some fuss with one of the punters not liking the show. He got held up over by the Top, sorting it out." His voice was gloomy, as if he was preparing for the worst. "I hope it doesn't put him in a rotten mood. I'm planning to show him my act once he's sorted it all."

"He'll give you a fair hearing. He's got to look to the future." Max could hear the bright edge to George's voice, and was sure he was trying to convince himself, as well as Loo-brush.

"I've got to prove my whole fun-mixed-with-fear performance will get him the publicity he wants."

"You've been practising like there's no tomorrow. He'll be amazed by you." George raised his thumb to Loo-brush. His voice was still bright. Almost forced. Max knew it was because he was worried about his own act. Hoping the guv'nor would be amazed by him too.

Loo-brush gave his tombstone smile again, before moving away along the carriages.

Max wondered what time it was. George had just guessed by the stars earlier, so it was no good asking him. Max needed to be sure it was past midnight when this ride through hell finished, otherwise he'd have to stay on board for a second go. Once midnight had passed, everyone would be safe.

The engine gave its ghoulish, moaning hoot. The train rattled forwards.

George slouched, his arms stretched casually along the back of the seat, not even holding the bar. Max hunched up even tighter, his own arms wrapped round himself. Hugging himself.

The engine moaned again. Then they clattered up the first loop. For a second, at the top, they almost stopped. Max felt his throat narrow. He couldn't swallow.

Meddy taste. Meddy taste.

He couldn't bring himself to look ahead, so he tried to relax by looking down at the park. It was still busy. Music thudded out from everywhere. The lights on the rides spun colours through the dark.

Max spotted Danior over by the mirror maze. The girl he was with had her yellow blonde hair pulled into a high, bouncy ponytail. They were eating out of scrunched up newspaper, and Danior must have annoyed her because she jerked her head up and wagged a cross finger at him. Danior laughed. She wagged her finger again, and this time Danior leant towards her, pushing her shoulder. The girl pushed him back. For a moment Max wondered if Danior was going to fight with her, but he didn't. Instead, he shrugged his shoulders and walked away. The girl hurled the scrunched up newspaper at his back, and a scatter of chips rained down onto the ground. Danior disappeared among a throb of people. The girl tossed her ponytail, stomping off in the other direction.

Max decided she must be the one Danior 'got lucky' with. It didn't look as if the luck had lasted very long. But there wasn't time to think any more. The train rushed forward, rocking and rattling.

Max thought he might wet his Spidermans after all. He dipped his head and tried closing his eyes, making himself concentrate. It didn't work any better here than in his real world life. He was spinning. Dizzy. Dizziness usually made him wake up. Perhaps the meddy tasting wasn't such a good idea after all. Max forced his eyes open again. The train reached the bottom, circling onto a wider track, coming level with the coconut stall.

Bibi hurried by, carrying a sleepy Patches. Clover loped along beside them, clutching the hem of Bibi's yellow dress.

"Hello, Bibi." The wobble-wide woman dangled a fluffy toy kitten at Bibi. "Come 'an 'ave a go now, like you promised."

Bibi paused, her face lit by the glittering lights. She was so close, Max wanted to reach out from the carriage and touch her. But then he remembered he couldn't touch anything. Helpless and hopeless.

"I'll be shuttin' up soon, darlin'. It's nearly midnight." The woman waved the kitten again. "Yer'll be doin' me a favour. I'll have one less prize to pack away when we finishes."

Bibi eyed the kitten eagerly, and then nodded. "I'll come back ever so soon, only I left Clover's jacket back by Sabre's wagon. Ma says the punters might get a bit cross about her scruffedy fur, so I'm just goin' to …"

The train was climbing again, and Max couldn't catch the last thing she said, but he could make a good enough guess.

Bibi must be heading back to get the jacket. Everything was how Barbara had remembered it. But it was all right. Nothing bad could happen as long as George was with him. And the coconut stall woman had said it was nearly midnight.

Max turned his attention back to the ride. The track grew steeper, and his breath felt trapped in his throat. The engine would never be strong enough. They would surely slide back down?

The train reached the highest point of the track. It hovered. Max wondered if he'd die in his sleep, gasping from fear. And then, across the moonless night, he heard bells.

One - two - three - four - five - six - seven - eight - nine - ten - eleven - twelve.

The last chime faded, and the fear faded too. Max was glowing. Burning inside a moment of brilliance. Amazing. Utterly, fantastically awesome.

It was gone midnight. He'd changed the past. Saved the future. He stretched his own arms along the back of the seat. George grinned at him, and Max grinned back.

Looking across to Sabre's trailer, he had a clear view of Bibi, walking away from the tent. She was still carrying Patches, who was all wrapped up and tucked inside her shawl. Clover was wearing her jacket. Max wanted to do backflips and handstands and juggle a zillion balls with his teeth. And then he froze. Just paces from Bibi, something white was stalking up behind her. The train surged forward. It rattled down the dip at the speed of death.

Max screamed his soundless scream, louder than anyone.

CAT ATTACK

The train slid back down, slowing as it edged back towards the beginning. Loo-brush was waving people away, telling them the ride was finished.

Max snatched hopelessly at George's sleeve, his hand passing through his arm.

George grinned. "Blimey, you look like you've seen a ghost. This ride has really shaken you up."

"How could you? I've just seen ..." Max was stumbling over his words. Shaking. Sick. "I saw it all from up there. You did it, didn't you? You unlocked the cage door. Sabre's escaped."

He lurched up and leapt out of the carriage even though it was still moving. Hurtling through the crowd, he rushed through people and tents and trailers and trucks without even seeing them. Without even thinking about it.

Bibi was still standing in the magical gold lamplight, smiling softly to herself, with Clover just behind. She shifted her hold on Patches and jiggled him gently. "Shhh, baby puppy. Sleep now. I'll keep yer safe all night."

Sabre had hunched into a crouched shadow. Flickering torchlight lit his eyes: dazzling, daggering, dangerously bright.

Max hurtled through Bibi and stood with his arms outstretched. His body made a useless invisible shield. Sabre's throat rumbled. His tail twitched. "No," begged Max. "Don't do it."

He was helpless. Despairing. He turned, frantic, looking for help. George was chasing up behind him. "Careful," he screamed. "Stop running."

George stopped. Stared ahead. His face drained of colour. "Bibi." He moved forward slowly, edging round the corner of the trailer and walking straight through Max. His voice was a hoarse whisper. "Stay very still. Trust me."

Bibi half turned towards him, "Shhh, Georgie. Patches is sleepin'."

"Don't move. Don't speak."

Sabre's eyes stayed fixed on Bibi.

Bibi turned back, saw – and understood. She drew a ragged intake of breath. Clover chattered, plucking anxiously at the hem of her dress. Patches woke up and squirmed in Bibi's arms. He tried to lick her face, wriggling and scrabbling his back legs. The shawl dropped away and Max could see his stumpy tail wagging wildly.

George's voice was urgent and low. "Put Patches down, Bibi, then step very carefully back towards me."

Bibi shook her head and held Patches tighter, drawing him into her chest. "No."

Patches wriggled even more. Sabre's eyes switched to watching the wagging tail.

"Bibi – you *have* to do what I say. It's the puppy, or you. There isn't any time. Put Patches on the ground. Give yourself a chance."

"I can't. Sabre will get him and hurt him. Please, Georgie … don't make me …"

But it was already too late. Sabre sprang. A blur of snarling white.

Bibi tumbled forward, knocked to the ground like a coconut. She hunched in a ball and tried to roll away, still clutching Patches. Clover screeched, jumping in a crazed circle around Bibi's huddled body.

Max watched in hopeless horror.

Sabre was on top of Bibi. His curled claws stretched out, scratching through her hair. The teeth George had battled so hard to save were locked onto her face. Blood trickled from her forehead, speckling the lamplit grass.

George crouched low, his face next to Sabre's. Max could see a vein throbbing in his neck. Clover was screeching so hard it took a moment for Max to hear what George was saying.

And then he got it.

"Die, Sabre, come on, boy. Die for the king." George's fingers ruffled the lion's mane. He stroked his ears, his voice always gentle. "Die for the king, Sabre. Die for the king." Max saw George's lips shape the sound of a silent whistle.

And it was as if a switch had been flicked. In that second

Sabre gave a soft growl, his claw dragging rags of blood across Bibi's face and neck. He rolled away from her onto his back, his blue eyes now dark with trust. Blinking up at George.

There were footsteps. Voices. "We are in the grip of great tragedy. Time is our enemy."

Max looked up to see the guv'nor hurtling towards them, one hand on his top hat, as if he was trying to ram it hard onto his head.

"The dreadful deed must be done. Make haste. Spare not a moment!" the guv'nor yelled.

And after him came Loo-brush. His powder white face glowed. His painted lips stretched into a terrible, blood-bright slash of red. The star-patterned trousers flapped strangely. A clown lurching across a nightmare, with one hand clutching a jewel studded knife.

Loo-brush threw as he ran.

The blade made an arc of silver across the dark.

WAKE-UP CALL

"Max? Max?"

Someone was calling but they seemed forever away. Max's eyes were locked open. He couldn't move and he couldn't speak but he could see. And what he could see was terrible.

Unbearable. Sabre lay where he'd rolled, his massive head drooped sideways. A dark, sticky line traced a red tear down one side of his face. A knife jutted out from above one blank, blue eye. The guv'nor kept shouting. Words spilling out of him. Jagged. Painful. Dredged with despair.

Max couldn't make out the detail of what he was saying.

George stood in front of the guv'nor, his hands crossed against his face as if the jagged words were weapons themselves. Max could see Loo-brush and he was hunched, rocking madly with Bibi in his arms. Bibi cried in harsh, painful sobs. Patches whined. There was a sad, quiet chattering.

And then everything blurred. The whole scene faded

away.

Max stared up at the sky and the moon was a giant silver penny.

"Max? Max?"

Barbara knelt beside me. I was back in real-time again, slumped against the knobbly tree.

"Save you," I whispered. "Sorry stop it. I couldn't. Couldn't sorry save you."

"I don't need saving, Max. No one's hurting me."

"Sabre wasn't locked. The door got you."

"I'm afraid you've had one of your silly dreams, dear. That's all. There's nobody here except you and me."

I tried to pull my thoughts together, speaking slowly. Concentrating on every word.

"I want stop the lion getting you. I wanted the scar face never hap-hap-happening."

"What has to be, has to be. No one can change the past." Barbara clutched a bunch of flowers. Their scent was peachy and sweet.

I struggled to make sense of everything, and the clearer it got, the sicker I felt.

George hadn't acted from a rush of anger when the guv'nor turned him down. That cage door must have been unlocked already, when I appeared out of nowhere. So he must have already talked to the guv'nor. Already been turned down earlier in the day. I hadn't tricked him into leaving the tent unguarded. He'd tricked me. He'd wanted me out the way because he knew that, if Sabre escaped while we were still sitting there, it wouldn't have been a problem. I'd have expected George to catch that lion easily, with all his clever tricks and whistles and words.

"Max, dear? You do look unwell. Is there anything I can do?"

I'd forgotten she was there. "W – why are you out here, in the d-d-dark?" I managed to stammer.

Her face was half shadowed, hiding the scar, but the moonlight touched her hair and dusted it silver. "I came for that cage boy. To see if I could forgive him." Her voice quivered. "I couldn't sleep, and kept trying to think kinder things about him, the way the asylum priest said I should. I thought it might help if I actually came out to the park, and tried to remember as much as I could. It was dark when I last saw George, you see, dear. Nearly midnight. He'd promised to look after the big cat while I went off to play. I was stood here, lost in old memories, when I heard you shout. I recognised your voice, so I came to find you."

"I don't think you have to forgive the cage boy," I said, and there was a bitter edge to my voice. "After all, he wanted to let the lion out. He may not have meant it to hurt you, but he knew what he was doing. You got it right the other day, when you said he did it out of spite. And that asylum priest probably never suffered in the ways that you have. He couldn't know how hard it's been for you, all these years. All the horrible things people have done to you."

It made me furious that she was risking the dark, trying to think kinder things about George. Karl, or Scuffer, or anyone bad, might come along and have a go at her.

Barmy Barbara
monster face
not part of
the human race

"That's very kind of you, Max." Her quivery voice was gentle. "I'm not sure that you're right, but I know you're just trying to protect me. Thank you again, dear." Barbara held out one frail hand to me. I took it, putting my other hand against the tree to pull myself up.

We stood awkwardly. Her skin was like dead leaves. I wanted it to be Bibi's hand I was holding. Bibi who I was leading away from my dream. But Barbara was right. You couldn't change the past. If you could just loop back through time and make bad things better, then people would be doing it every day. I felt very wise suddenly. Wiser than Jamil. And achingly sad.

"Shall we go home?" I said.

We shuffled at Barbara's pace.

I still couldn't get over that George had been so calculating. Cold blooded. He'd been waiting for Sabre to escape.

He must have been really hacked-off when I'd turned up. I raked my mind back over all the fake things he'd said, and how he pretended to be upset about never seeing me again. How he'd somehow goaded me into saying we ought to go on the roller coaster. George. My only friend ever. *How could he, how could he?*

We walked out through the gate and down Smithson Street, past the crammed together houses and the stinky flats.

There was a scrunched up chip wrapper in the gutter and I kicked it. It rolled a few feeble metres and then stopped. I've never been great at kicking a ball.

And then I remembered something else.

I got a hazed memory of the girl with the ponytail chucking her chips at Danior's back. The memory grew stronger. New images spun and hooted and whirled. It was hard to slow them down. Hard to get a proper look at them. But they were important. There was something more I needed to make clearer. I had glimpses of the girl storming away ... and pictures of Danior. There was something I needed to remember about Danior. Some vital detail. I had to grab control of this memory.

Lucid waking.

Suddenly, it hit me.

Danior was at the fair just before midnight, even though he'd told George he wouldn't be. He'd had time, once he left the girl, to get across to the tent. And Danior had lots of reasons for wanting George to be in big, big trouble.

It made perfect sense. Danior had set George up. He'd been framed.

I felt a rush of new energy fizz through me. I couldn't change the past - I didn't even want to any more. But I could do something about the present. I could put things right for everyone who was still alive. "That cage boy you've been trying to forgive," I said shakily. "Perhaps you've been doing the right thing after all. D'you know what happened to him?"

FACING THE FUTURE

"This is it. The wonderful Lion-Land. Are you feeling all right, Barbara?"

Miss Kindly took her hand off the steering wheel and touched Barbara's arm. "I still can't believe you know this marvellous man who set all this up."

Barbara nodded but she didn't speak.

As we drove under the arched entrance, I wondered how the day ahead was going to go.

My dreams had all stopped. The doctors announced there was nothing wrong with me. I was back at school. Even Mr Snook said he was 'pleased with my progress'. Everything was good, except for this one last thing I needed to put right.

The private road beyond the archway ran past fields. It dipped round a bend. There were more fields. A gate. A small sort of sentry box.

Miss Kindly opened her window and said something to a cheery faced man who came out of the sentry box to greet us. He checked a list, nodded, and waved us through.

We passed a long wooden building with a grass roof and a sign saying:

Restaurant: A Taste of Africa

There was a gift shop at the far end.

Miss Kindly turned into a drive marked

'PRIVATE'.

We drew up outside a white, pillared, mansion, where yellow roses climbed across the walls between the arched windows, and stone steps led to the heavy wooden door.

"Well, here we are." Miss Kindly smiled round at us, and we all clambered out.

Barbara let out a small, quavering breath. "It all looks so grand."

"It's part of a Trust. I'm not sure how much Max has told you, but Mr Freeman – that's your old friend George – initially got a job here as a groundskeeper. But then Lord Toogood, who owned the estate, couldn't afford the upkeep any more. George Freeman had heard of some circus lions that were being ill-treated and he somehow convinced Lord Toogood about the idea of a sanctuary. It was the first of its kind in this country. George Freeman was a man ahead of his time."

Ahead of his time.

It felt weird, hearing Miss Kindly say that.

He was more ahead of his time than she would ever know.

It was Jamil who'd found him for me. He'd googled 'George' and 'Lions' and it had all flashed onto the screen of his iPhone as if it had been just waiting for someone to click the right link.

Sophie even cried when she realised George ran the same 'Lion-Land' that Miss Kindly was always going on about.

It was Sophie that persuaded Miss Kindly to set up a meeting for me and Barbara.

There was an extension built on the left side of the mansion, and Miss Kindly linked her arm through Barbara's and pointed to it. "I'm afraid we won't get to go in the big house though. Mr Freeman's quarters are over here. Come on. He's expecting us."

My stomach squirmed. Barbara had come to put the past 'to rest'. She still thought it was George who let Sabre out, but she was ready to forgive him. She'd decided he'd been angry and hot-headed, and had just made a stupid young boy's mistake. I'd listened to her talk it all through, and felt swollen with secrets. Longing to tell her. But Sophie and Jamil said I had to talk to George. I had to find out what he thought was best.

The office door opened. An old man shuffled out. His grey mane of hair still reached to his shoulders.

"Bibi – I can't quite believe it's you, after all these years …" His voice had that old person croak, but behind it I could still hear the gentleness. He put one hand out to touch her, his eyes searching her face. Not flinching. Not shocked or horrified or scared. But I could see he was hurting. His green eyes - still those same gold flecks – looked clouded with sadness. "Come into my office. Come in."

He led us through the open door. I felt my ears pinking up as I followed them all through. What would happen? What did I even want?

A dark haired girl in green wellingtons appeared from behind another door. "I thought you'd appreciate tea while you chatted, Grandad." She smiled as she wedged the tray down onto the paper-piled table.

"Thanks, Ruby." George glanced at Barbara as if he was half expecting her to start shouting at him as soon as we were all settled. Maybe he even wanted her to do that. Maybe he thought he deserved it. "Much appreciated."

"I'll leave you in peace now." Ruby smiled again. "But if any of you want a look round, just shout. I'll take you to where our new tigers are, and then we can drive one of the safari vans round the main fields."

"The tigers are Ruby's newest project." George nodded at her, then threw a worried glance at Barbara again. "She rescued them from a temple in Thailand. They were about to be sold for their skins. Ruby convinced me we should look further than lions in our rescue packages. We cover everything now. I think we'd have the Dodo bird if it still existed."

"And a woolly mammoth." Ruby smiled at him, then

hesitated, her hand on the door. "Performing wild animals are pretty much gone from this country now, but there are still plenty of places where terrible things happen." Her eyes widened for a moment, and I wasn't sure if she was suddenly angry, or trying not to cry. Maybe it was both.

She shook her head, as if she wanted to shake whatever she was feeling away. "For instance, there are tragic stories of dancing bears in some parts of the world. Little cubs are stolen from their mums, have their noses drilled and ropes pushed through them—that's what makes them dance— the pain of the rope being pulled against the wound. We send money to a programme that buys them off their owners. And it's not just poor countries that are cruel and thoughtless. We're going to have a couple of chimps soon too. A celebrity with more money than sense - I can't tell you her name – she got them for her daughter, only the chimps got fleas and the daughter refused to go near them. They've been locked in a garage for over a year. One way or another, we help as many suffering animals as ..." She smiled suddenly, her face softening. "Sorry. I tend to get a bit carried away. You didn't come here for a lecture."

"I used to have a baby chimp," Barbara said quietly. "It was when I was little. I'm afraid I didn't realise there was anything bad about keeping her then. I suppose I was wrong, dear."

"We try to educate children about things like that here." Ruby nodded at Barbara. "They can't learn what they're not taught. And it breaks my heart, in a way, that we've got this place at all. In my perfect world, all wild animals should be left alone."

Barbara clasped her fingers together, speaking sadly. "I can see why it's had to change. Our trainers didn't mean to be cruel, but I'm sure the animals were often miserable. Even my little chimp would never have chosen the life she had." She shook her head. "I do wish I could slip back through time and put things right for her. But I suppose I was so very young then, and even if I'd thought like that, no one would have listened to me anyway, dear."

Ruby patted Barbara on the shoulder. "You're right. No one knew any better back then." She smiled round at us all.

"I must go and organise the feeds for this afternoon, but hopefully I'll catch up with you later." She waved as she left the office.

"Perhaps you could adopt one of those newly rescued chimps from here? Just like I've done with my lion. We can't change the past, but we can change the future." Miss Kindly beamed at Barbara, then turned to me. "You've seen pictures of my lion haven't you, Max? I'm hoping to take more today."

George glanced at me for the first time.

I saw him jolt. His face turned ghost pale.

An eternity of time ticked between us.

Then he raised one eyebrow. "You look like someone I used to know."

I battled to raise one eyebrow back. "You look like someone I used to know too."

TRUTH TIME

It was Miss Kindly and Barbara who went off with Ruby.

They drank the tea and George told them about Lion-Land and Barbara kept looking at him and smiling. I could see she was trying to let him know she'd forgiven him. George looked tense, but I wasn't sure if it was because of Barbara, or me. He seemed relieved when Miss Kindly said she'd like to take up the offer of having a look around. He called Ruby on her mobile, and she came back to collect them.

I invented a sudden headache, and George twigged in to what I was up to. He said he'd take me upstairs to his flat so I could have a rest.

Miss Kindly agreed immediately. "Max has been ill," she told George. "We need to be careful." She held one arm out to Barbara, and together they bustled along behind Ruby, following her back outside.

"Sit down," George said, as soon as we were up in his flat. "I need to sit too. I know I'm ancient, but my legs have never felt so much like buckling before. I wasn't even sure

I'd make it up the stairs."

I sat in a big, sand coloured armchair.

He sank into the seat opposite, not taking his eyes off me. "I've never forgotten you. I've never stopped looking for clues about you." He pressed his gnarled up fingers against his forehead. His skin was mottled brown. The skin of someone who has spent their life working outdoors. "You made a difference to me. I had the idea about this place because of something you said about animals being caged. You made me see how wrong it was, and I wanted to do something right. I thought I could make life better for captive big cats, so at least Sabre didn't die in vain. I've always wanted to at least find your grave, to thank you. But you always insisted you weren't dead, and now you're here. What's happened? Or is it just my increasingly fuddled brain playing tricks on me?"

"I'll explain later. As best I can. Though I'm not sure if you'll believe me."

George frowned and rubbed his head with the back of his hand. "I'll believe you," he said softly, "because I trust you and because I *want* to believe you – like I've just said, I've always tried to find a way to thank you."

I felt awkward. We were friends, except he was an old man and I was just a few weeks older than the last time I saw him. Now he was telling me he'd opened up Lion-Land because of things I'd said.

I tried to keep focused on what had happened that terrible night. "I thought I'd done a bad thing to you. I thought it was me who'd given you the idea to set Sabre free."

George didn't seem to be able to pull his gaze away from me. He shook his head. "I've been haunted by such terrible memories. I've tried to honour the memory of Sabre with this place, but Bibi is a different matter. How could I ever put things right for her?"

I sat forward in my chair, suddenly not awkward any more. "You got blamed, didn't you? Everyone said you let Sabre out on purpose."

"I don't know what they said, because I ran away. I was good at that. But trust me, Max, I didn't let him loose on purpose. I was careless. Which is still unforgivable. But Sabre was one clever cat. I'd been so busy planning what I was going to say to the guv'nor, I must have forgotten to lock the cage door. It was a rickety old thing, and Sabre liked to rub his head against it. It's my belief it just pushed open, and he trotted out. Poor boy probably couldn't believe his luck."

I fixed my eyes on his, speaking slowly to make sure I was being very clear. "What if you *had* locked it, but someone unlocked it again later?"

"Not possible. It's all etched in my mind. Danior was off out with some fancy girl he'd picked up. I was the last one in that tent. It was all down to me."

"Except ... Danior came back. I saw him from the top of the roller coaster ride." I was watching George's face. "He had an argument with that girl, she stormed off. Danior headed away towards the tent. It must have only been about

227

five minutes before Sabre got Bibi."

I saw shadows moving across George's eyes. Memories. Nightmares.

I was seeing them too.

"You're saying I didn't do it? You're saying it was Danior?"

"You probably saved Bibi. If you hadn't got there, and if you hadn't made Sabre stop …"

He held up one hand as if he couldn't cope with hearing any more, squeezing his eyes shut. I wondered if he was going to cry. I wondered if I was. "Danior died recently. He'd tried to get Barbara to visit him in this care home he'd ended up in – I don't know why he wanted to see her. Perhaps he wanted to tell her the truth at last. Perhaps the guilt was too much even for him." I paused for breath. I had so much to say, and it was all rolling out of me like a runaway train. "But anyway, Barbara didn't go. Both Danior and her mum left her to rot in that mental asylum, and she struggled to forgive them for that. They never even visited. But once she got the letter saying Danior had died, she felt bad that she'd never made herself go and see him one last time. And she kept going back to the woods, those ones where the asylum used to be. She kept remembering that week – her last happy times before it all happened. Re-living them over and over in her head."

George kept his eyes on me. I'd forgotten how good he was at just keeping on looking, but my ears didn't flush up this time. I kept rattling on. "Have you ever heard of a bloke called Einstein? He's got something to do with time-loops and stuff. My mate Jamil thinks –"

"Grandad?" Ruby called from the bottom of the stairs. "How's Max now? His teacher says that if he's feeling better she'll take him out to see Petra's puppies. She says it would be a shame for him not to see *some* sort of animal while he's here. You and Barbara can have another cup of tea on your own together."

George hesitated a moment, then called down, "Of course, sweetheart. We're on our way."

As I stood up, I said in a rush, "Are you going to tell Barbara. Do you want me to try and explain?"

From down in the office I could hear Barbara and Miss Kindly chattering. They both sounded excited, as if seeing the animals had made them into children again.

"No." George gave a sharp shake of his head. "We won't tell her. It's bad enough that it happened. How much worse will it be if she has to think her own brother caused it? And Danior's gone, so even if he was about to come clean on it all, he's lost that last chance. There's no need to hurt her any more, now. Let her still believe it was me. Don't give her any new pain. The main thing is that I know. You don't know how much grief and guilt has been lifted off me." His eyes twinkled suddenly. "I feel almost your age again."

As he led me back through to join the others in his office, he went to the corner, reaching for something that was on the top of a grey metal cabinet. It was a toy. A slightly dusty brown bear. "I tried to give this to someone special, a long time ago, but he couldn't take it. Maybe you could look after it instead?" He threw it gently.

I caught it, easily.

Then he stretched out his weathered hand. "You'll be back, I hope. Or I'll drop in on you if young Bibi here ever invites me to sample her home cooking."

He winked at Bibi and she twisted a smile at him.

"That's great." I grinned. "Maybe you can tell me all about life in a travelling circus; the way it was when you really *were* my sort of age'."

He raised one eyebrow. "Ah, now that's something you and me can probably chat about for ever."

We shook hands like grown ups.

His grip was strong. Firm.

And very real.

TIME AFTER TIME

"I can't wait for the new skate park to be built. They're starting work in September." Jamil rattles down the ramp on his newest super-kryptonite board.

Sophie straightens the ramp and adds a sheet of ridged metal at the back. "Well done you for sorting that petition, and working with the council to make it all happen. It'll be brilliant. Mum says it might even stop the next generation of thugs." She steps aside and watches Jamil skate a little way along the path, and then skim back for another go. "Everyone can burn off their negative energy at the park, and stay out of trouble. Negative energy can destroy the soul. Mum's been learning about this thing called feng shui, and explaining it to me."

I flop down on the grass. It's way too hot to keep rushing around collecting planks and bits of metal. Scamp bounces over and begins chewing my laces. "Hey, little puppy, it took me ages to tie those right this morning." I reach down to scratch his silly brown ears.

"I wonder how my mum's getting on with your dad."

Sophie flops beside me. "I can't believe he set up a lunch date with her."

"Don't get too excited. He's probably taking her for a triple cheeseburger and fries."

Sophie giggles. "You're wrong. Barbara's cooked for them." She sits forward, hugging her knees. "She wanted to thank my mum for sorting her hair out, so she's done some sort of herby vegetarian casserole and given it to your dad to heat."

I see Scuffer and Gabby saunter up to the gate.

Karl Blade is in prison, and Sophie thinks they're keeping their heads down. She heard it was Scuffer who blagged about where Madam Cream's things were hidden. He struck some kind of deal with the police to save his own skin.

Sophie thinks they know they went too far that day at Barbara's. They're scared I might do some blagging of my own. She's certain they'll leave me alone from now on.

I am trying my best to believe her, but I keep one eye on them both, just in case.

They see me looking, and walk away.

Scamp bounces onto my chest and begins licking my face. "Get off me." I push him away, but I'm laughing.

He rolls over and Sophie tickles his puppy pink tummy. "Have you booked up for those dog training classes yet?"

"They start next Saturday." I tickle his tummy too.

Jamil skims past us. "Watch this stunningly choreographed powerslide with backflip," he calls. "If I can get it right, it'll seem like I'm defying the laws of physics."

"We're watching." Sophie pulls Scamp onto her lap and waves his paw at Jamil.

Jamil waves back.

Scamp isn't one of Patches' great-great-grandpuppies – that would have been too much of a perfect ending. George doesn't know what happened to Patches, but he says the travellers' life was always pretty good for a dog. They could usually roam free. There were plenty of show-people around who liked animals. And there was always lots going on.

Scamp is one of Ruby's dog's puppies. It was Miss Kindly who persuaded Dad that having him would be good for me. And with Barbara insisting she'd come over and puppy-sit for parts of the day, Dad couldn't come up with a reason to say no.

Scamp squirms round, chewing Sophie's fingers. "Ouch! Your doggy is bored," she giggles.

"I'll race him." I jump up and attempt my wonky whistle. I'm getting better at it. George has been teaching me. Maybe one day I'll be good enough to manage a pitch that's so special, only dogs can hear.

"Come on, boy. Last one to the woods is a wimp."

And I run, Scamp bouncing round me and barking, both of us chasing across to the trees where the summer sun pours light across the branches.

WORDTAMER

ROLL UP, ROLL UP

MASTER THE SKILLS AND THRILLS OF
TAMING WORDS TO TELL STORIES OF YOUR
OWN WITH ALL THE DRAMA, PASSION
AND SKILL OF A PROFESSIONAL WRITER.

Tricks and Tips:
Creative Writing Training

Good wordtamers often use note books to help them, so get one ready, and use it as a training ground for your writing and ideas.

1. Brave Beginnings
2. Capturing Character
3. Death Defying Dialogue
4. Grappling with Genre
5. Snaring a Setting
6. Prowling through Plot
7. Stalking Show not Tell
8. Wild, Wild Words
9. Pouncing on Point of View
10. Endings to Die For
11. Bite Size Treats and Snacks of Ideas

BRAVE BEGINNINGS

Ever heard the phrase "you only get one chance to make a first impression"? That works in writing stories too.

The first page – first paragraph – first sentence – are the 'claw' where wordtamers make their story powerful from the start.

If wordtamers don't grab their reader in those early moments, the reader may just slip away, and make their escape towards somebody else's story.

But what does the wordtamer mean by a 'claw'?

Here is the beginning from Funfear:
I stared, almost hypnotised. A little girl stood between the trees that guarded the far end of the park. She was a long way off, but she seemed to be staring straight back at me. And there was something wrong. Something strange about her.

From this beginning, readers know that something strange, or even spooky, is happening.
  This is the 'claw' – the aim is to grab the reader's interest, so that they are hungry to know what happens next.

WORDTAMER TRAINING: Get a picture in your head of
how your story might begin. Think about the main
characters. Where are they? Is there anything strange,
or unusual, or exciting, about what is happening?

Jot down notes in your 'training' book. Try and picture the
early scenes in your imagination *before* you start on the actual
story.

Once you think you've pictured that beginning with as much
detail as possible, you are ready to grab your reader –**think for
a moment – are you using any of the following 'claws' in
your paragraph?**

Horror ● Terror ● Excitement ● Danger ● Mystery

If none of the above feels right for your idea, see if you can
come up with a 'claw' of your own.

**Once you think you've worked out some 'grabbing'
possibilities, write the first sentence of your story, then
read it out loud. If the words feel as if they would claw
your reader in, then just keep going and see where the
idea takes you.**

*Lots of fantastic stories have been written by
wordtamers who start a first sentence and then keep
chasing words all the way through to the end.*

Capturing Character

Good wordtamers need to learn as much as they can about their characters, so that they know how they might behave in their story. In the early scenes from Funfear, rough notes were scratched out about Max, Sophie and Jamil.

Here are the notes for Max:

Character name:
Max Baxter

What he looks like:
Skinny, a bit pale.

What might matter to him?
Wants to be liked (particularly by Sophie)

What things might be hard for him?
Gets in trouble a lot. He's an outsider

What background detail is there about him?
Lives with his Dad, Mum died when Max was quite small. Max was fostered out when he was younger because Dad was unemployed and not coping well, but Max has been allowed to return home now that Dad has found work.

They live in a two bedroom old style terrace house in a small town that is a bit scruffy.

WORDTAMER TRAINING: Capture a character by jotting notes in your training book about the following details:

A character's name

What they look like

What sorts of things matter to them?

What sorts of things might they hate, or are scared of?

What other notes can you make about where they live, or who they live with?

By pinning down these snippets of information, you will be capturing details that will help your character feel 'real' to you. And if they feel real to you, your reader will believe in them too.

Scratch down story ideas that might go with this character. Lots of fantastic stories have been written by wordtamers who capture a character, then set up a story around them.

DEATH-DEFYING DIALOGUE

Dialogue is all about when characters start to speak. In a way, it belongs with the 'character' pages, because a good wordtamer knows that they need to develop the character first, and then dialogue is easy.

Once a wordtamer knows who the character is, they know the sorts of things they say, and the ways they will say it.

In Funfear, Loo-brush is always gloomy. Danior is always angry or nasty. Miss Kindly is always caring.

Of course – it gets more complicated than that. In real life, no one is (usually) gloomy or nasty or caring all the time. And in good writing, wordtamers need their characters to feel real. But working out some of the key behaviours about a character *will* help the dialogue to sound right.

And remember, dialogue is usually placed between **❝small strange flying beasts called speech marks❞**

WORDTAMER TRAINING: Learn to make your characters feel 'real' whenever they speak.

Here is a list of possible character 'types:

Bossy ● Lazy ● Sulky ● Cruel ● Nervous ● Greedy.

Which three 'types' has the wordtamer used in the following scene?

"I'm scared of roller coasters," said Peter.

"Oh, don't be such a wimp." Laura gave him a sharp poke with her finger.

"He doesn't have to go on it if he doesn't want to." John was eyeing the hot dog stall opposite. "Why don't we all go *and grab some food instead.*"

Make notes in your training book. Capture three new characters from the types above. Choose names and ages. Scratch down notes about what they look like.

Write a scene where each of your characters speaks at least twice. Try to let their mood come out in the things they say.

You can add action to the dialogue, like in this scene from Funfear:

"You stupid josser." Danior spoke <u>through gritted teeth</u>. "Think you can nick my new act?"

Wordtamers sometimes write plays or even scripts for films. Could you do this with the dialogue ideas you've been training?

GRAPPLING WITH GENRE

The main genres in Funfear could be described as Science Fiction (time-slip) and Mystery. The time-slip sets up a mystery which links the past and the present, with lots of action and pace. It also has touches of 'Historical' and 'Thriller'.

Below are some of the main genres in story-writing.

Ghost – anything ghostly or ghoulish.
Thriller – lots of action, often with spies or politics.
Historical - set in the past. (Needs lots of research – wordtamers need to always get their facts right).
Fantasy – dragons, princes/princesses, magical things.
Science Fiction – machines, robots, planets and aliens.
Mystery – strange goings on.
Romance – in love, out of love, boy meets girl.
Horror – blood and gore and torture and death.
Crime – detectives, villains and criminals, who dunnits.
Contemporary: urban – everyday real life problems and gritty situations.

WORDTAMER TRAINING: Grapple with genre, to see what new ideas start scrabbling through your imagination.

Below are some examples of the sort of genre based sentence a wordtamer might write:

Ghost: A misted figure drifted by, moaning sadly.
Fantasy: A unicorn danced by a silver fountain.
Sci-Fi: The space-sub hovered, fixing its position.
Horror: His eye burst and green sludge oozed out.
Crime: PC Marley saw the boot before he saw the body.
Urban: The tramp stumbled across the broken glass.

Scratch a sentence in your notebook for one of the following genres:

Ghost ● Fantasy ● Sci-Fi ● Horror ● Crime ● Urban

You may get story ideas from just that one sentence. If so, then just keep going. If not, choose your favourite sentence from the list above, and see if you can carry on an idea from that.

Wordtamers often choose to write the sort of stories they like reading themselves. They choose genres they are drawn to. What sorts of books do you like? What sort of genres are they? Once you've decided, do some research to find out as much about that genre as possible.

SNARING A SETTING

Wordtamers see the setting as the backdrop to the story. Some of them describe it as being like the stage scenery in a play. They know it is important to understand where the story is set, and to show the characters against this setting

But this doesn't mean they use loads of description - just a few details and carefully placed words can 'paint the scene'.

In the following extract from Funfear readers can see where Max is, and what the weather is like.

I was out in the street, round the other side of the park and outside the chip shop. The shop was closed but a bag of chips lay squished on the pavement. Flies muzzed round it. The air was warm but it didn't smell of peaches. Or even chips. I stared up at the sky. There were no clouds. The day was glittery bright and the sky stretched an endless blue.

Below are examples of settings a wordtamer might scratch down early ideas about:

City? Village? Town?
Buildings (what type?)
Fields (long or short grass? Marshy? Crops or flowers?)
Mountains (Snowy? Icy? Jagged? In the clouds?)
The Sea (Calm or stormy? Deep or shallow?
Desert? Jungle? Forest?

WORDTAMER TRAINING: Scratch down some notes to decide where your story might be set. Imagine what it might look like if it were a film, or a play.

Will your idea will be set in the past, present or future?

Decide:

Where? Field, Forest, Sea, River, Town, City, Desert.

When? Time of year, Time of day …

Weather? Hot, cold, windy, snowy, rain-lashed …

Any other details?

Good wordtamers often don't start their story properly until they have the setting clear in their heads.

Once you've scratched down your notes, spend a minute thinking about your character walking up to the scene, and moving around inside it. Think about something happening … is it something scary, or dangerous, or exciting?

As soon as you know, then start writing – see how much you can write. Some wordtamers find a whole story will come to them just by thinking up settings.

PROWLING THROUGH PLOT

An idea is just that—an idea. It isn't a story. Wordtamers know that if they take an early idea, and then work out a plot, it starts to be a story.

The early idea for Funfear was of a time slip that involved a boy called Max, and animals in travelling fairs.
The plot was harder to write—and it kept changing.

This is a simple Funfear plot:
    Max has no friends. He is bored.
    He slips through to another time.
    He makes his first true friend ever.
    He tries to help his friend, but everything goes wrong.
    Max finds a new way to help his friend.
    Max finds new friends in his 'real life' time.

Some wordtamers draw maps to help them 'see' the way the story might work.

Some write lists, scribbling what happens next …
… and next … and next.

Some don't plot at all – they just write, and see where the writing takes them.

Whatever way a wordtamer chooses to plot their idea, they try to keep possibilities open – if a better idea comes along, good wordtamers are always willing to change their minds.

WORDTAMER TRAINING: **Simple tricks can get plot ideas started. You might want to tame the wordtamer idea, or you might want to train a new plot of your own.**

Wordtamer idea: Read the plot and then write the story:

Dray is a ten year old boy. The genre is fantasy. The setting is a spooky circus with strange 'freakish' creatures.

Dray has a pet dragon that he wants to keep secret.
A dragon would be valuable in a 'freak animal show'.
A girl discovers Dray's dragon. She blackmails Dray.
Dray gets in danger because of the girl's demands.
There is more trouble. The girl gets in danger too.
The dragon saves the girl. They all become friends.
They rescue all the 'freak' animals and go somewhere safe.

Train your own plot: First make notes about character, genre and setting.

Next, scratch down:
A problem, secret, or something the character wants.
Who, or what, might cause trouble?
What could happen next?
What might your character do about it?
How could things get worse?
What might your character do to solve everything?
How could the story end?

Most wordtamers find the story gets more interesting once they actually start to write it, but they can go back and check the plot if they get stuck.

STALKING SHOW NOT TELL

This is 'advanced' wordtamer training, so skip it if you don't feel ready yet – but it seems worth putting in a couple of pages about it for those who feel ready to have a go.

It's OK to use a mix of 'showing' and 'telling' in your writing, but stories that are ALL 'telling' are usually a bit boring.

Look at the difference between these two scenes:

Telling: Max stood watching the waltzers. They were very colourful. They spun fast. The ride made a hooting noise, which was scary. Max thought that the people on the ride looked worried.

Showing: Max watched the waltzers as they spun past, their colours blurring. Raising his hands to his ears, he tried to blot out the eerie hooting that ran a cold chill through his heart. A carriage whirled past him and he glimpsed a woman's face, wide eyed and pale.

A good wordtamer will use action mixed with description to 'show' their scenes, rather than just 'tell' what is going on.

WORDTAMER TRAINING: Choose a character, and a place.
Think of some scene that your character is standing in.
Scratch a few simple notes in your training book.

Keep the notes simple. Don't worry about making them interesting. They don't need to be interesting yet.

Write down: **Who the character is. Where they are.
What is happening around them. What they might be
feeling.**

Here is an example, if you're not sure:

Liam—in a town—a strange alien bird is flying around—Liam is scared

Look at your notes, then write a paragraph using action and description to <u>show</u> how the character is part of the scene, and also to <u>show</u> what they are feeling.

**You can let your writing run free now, and use exciting
or dramatic words.**

Example: Liam ducked down an alley between the shops as the creature dived again, its alien beak open, snatching people as they ran. Liam heard the screams but didn't stop to look back. His heart hammered as he ran.

Good wordtamers always look back over their writing and see if they can bring it to life more – and 'showing' rather than 'telling' is a powerful way for them to do this.

*Read through what you've written, and see if you can
change anything to bring in even more action, or to
make the scene more dramatic or powerful.*

WILD, WILD WORDS

Sometimes wordtamers like to write without thinking, and see what happens. Wild writing can set free wonderful ideas.

Wordtamers sometimes write like this if they're feeling stuck, or if they're trying to create a powerful or important scene.

They start with a word or a sentence – any words that feel important to their story, and start writing.

The following sample of wild writing was used in Funfear – it starts as an experiment, catching three words and scratching them down:

Silver ● Moon ● Lion

The three words were trained to become a paragraph:
The silver moon hangs like a penny. The branches of the trees make patterns against the night. A magic lion is hidden behind the darkness.

The paragraph was trained to become part of Funfear:
The moon hung like a huge silver penny. The branches of the trees scratched crazy patterns against the night. A wind sprang up and shivered the leaves … I stared at the moon, and tried to see Sabre's eyes staring back, blue-fire magic against the silver. The lion in the moon. I kept whispering the words over and over, the lion in the moon, the lion in the moon.

WORDTAMER TRAINING: Have a go at training your
own wild writing. See what happens. The results are
sometimes magical and you might be amazed!

Choose ONE word from these wild words below, capture it
by copying it into your training book, then scratch down two
more of your own.

Floating ● Jagged ● Fizzing ● Lost ● Wonderland

Hideous ● Lonely ● Jewel ● Magic ● Creak

**Spend a minute or two just looking at the three words
you've written. Let your imagination get used to them.
Then, when you're ready, start writing something –
anything – connected with these words.**

You might find your ideas start running wild, and you'll have
to chase after them with your pen as they come spilling down
out of your imagination.

*Wordtamers not only want to think of new and original
stories – they want to use words in different and
exciting ways inside those stories. Taming wild words is
one way for them to get this to happen.*

CORNERING CLIFF﹏HANGERS

Exciting …

…dangerous…

…shocking, chilling and terrifying.

Cliffhangers are usually used at the end of chapters – particularly an action filled chapter where there is loads happening. They are a powerful trick for wordtamers. They make the story feel fast paced. They keep the reader turning the page. They can even stop readers going to sleep at night, because they feel they have to keep reading. They have to know what will happen next.

Funfear has lots of 'cliffhanger' chapter endings.

Example 1: The rat-bat crate seemed to shiver. To tremble. And something was climbing out.

Example 2: "NO!"
The lion sprang.

Example 3: Max screamed his soundless scream, louder than anyone.

In each one, something dramatic seems about to happen.

WORDTAMER TRAINING: Have a go at using cliff hangers to start whole new stories. Look at the three 'dramatic' sentences below.

1: He closed his eyes, and jumped.
2: Something was creeping up behind her.
3: And then came the scream …

Choose one of these, and scratch it down into your training book.

Jot down some notes about what YOU think the chapter might have been about.

Then write the chapter idea that YOU have invented, and end it with the cliffhanger that you chose. You might write a paragraph, a chapter – or maybe even a whole book with loads more cliff-hanger type chapters.

There are all sorts of tricks wordtamers can do with cliffhangers. They can 'tease' the reader by not carrying on straight away what happens next. Or they can use a 'false' cliffhanger, to give pace to their story. The sentence seems dramatic, but once the reader rushes to the next chapter, it turns out to be something normal - this time …

POUNCING ON POINT-OF-VIEW

Point-of-View (known as POV) means that the whole story is told from just <u>one</u> character's viewpoint.

By using a single POV in a story, wordtamers can make sure the reader is clear who to care about, and who to worry about. If the reader cares about the main character, they will want to get to the end of the story.

In Funfear, Max is the main POV:

Max tilted his fingers back towards George. He could see George's hand tremble, as if he was straining for something. Waiting for something. George's eyes were green. There were gold flecks in the centers, like a scattering of glitter. Max felt weird being stared at for so long. He wanted to look away, but thought George might think he was rude.

He could feel his ears flushing up pink. They always did that when he got embarrassed.

Here is the same scene from Georges' POV:

George could feel his hands tremble as Max reached towards him. The ghost boy kept staring, his pale face suddenly pink with a soft blush. George had never thought about ghosts getting embarrassed before – but then again, he hadn't thought about ghosts much at all. Not until now.

Funfear would be a very different story if it had been told from Georges' POV, even though the plot would be the same.

WORDTAMER TRAINING: Writing stories from a single POV is a wordtamer skill worth mastering. But it's not always clear, before the writing starts, who the main character of a story is. There might be two, or more, who want to sign up for the part!

Story idea: One afternoon a boy and a girl go for a walk in the woods. The boy is the nervous type. The girl is bossy. The woods get thicker. Darker. Then out of the darkness a crumbling building looms up in front of them. It has towers and turrets. It is grown over with weeds and ivy. The place feels silent, and very eerie.

Choose a name and an age for each character, and scratch it down in your training book.

Write a paragraph about finding the building, and walking around it, from the nervous boys' <u>first person</u> POV.

Write a paragraph about exactly the same things, only from the bossy girls' <u>first person</u> POV.

Notice the differences in the writing. And notice, too, whether one felt easier to write than the other.

Sometimes something spooky happens when wordtamers do this. The writing around one character feels stronger. It's as if they are asking to be chosen. If this happens, trust them. Write the story with them as the main character. They probably have the most interesting part to play in your story, and they are hungry for you to get it written down.

Endings to Die For

Good wordtamers always want to write an unforgettable ending. The last sentence is as important as the first.

Funfear has an 'aaah factor' ending. Everything is explained. The reader can see that, although there are still possible problems, lots of the things in Max's life are better than they were at the start. This is a popular way to end a story.

There are others. Good wordtamers know how to tame and train all of them.

What about if the story ends on a cliff hanger? Readers will be rushing to buy the next book in the series.

What about a tragic ending, where the main character doesn't end up happy, or even dies?

What about twisting the ending, so that the character who seemed to be the 'good guy' turns out to be an evil wicked baddie – or the other way round?

What about taking the reader back round to the beginning? Everything *seems* to be sorted, but as the character returns to that scene from the start, something new happens. The poor character may have to start all over again (although usually in another book, of course). This is known as a 'circular' story.

WORDTAMER TRAINING: Scratch down ONE sentence for each of the following types of ending. It doesn't matter if you have no idea how the story starts – just think how it might end.

An 'aaaah factor' happy ending.

A cliff hanger ending.

A sad or tragic ending.

A twist in the tale ending.

A circular story ending.

Often, when a wordtamer tames and trains words for an ending, they suddenly discover a fresh herd of words, all galloping about looking for a new story. If that happens to you, go back to Brave Beginnings, and tame and train your own new story ideas – then you really will be working like a professional wordtamer.

BITE SIZE TREATS AND SNACKS OF IDEAS

STORMING THROUGH STYLE: Wordtamers often experiment with style early on in their idea. Would the story work better in first person, or third person? Present tense, or past tense? Look back at Funfear - it uses first person for the chapters when Max is in his 'normal' life, and third person when he slips into the past. Notice, too, that the last chapter is different again – this time it's in the present tense. Early wordtamers often struggle with tenses, so have another look at the examples in Funfear, to understand them properly, and then try them yourself.

There are other tricks too – could your story be told as a diary, or through blogs or emails? Could it be narrated by an extra character who is looking back at what happened? Could you include poems and rhymes? Riddles? Quizzes? Maps? There are lots of extra ways to tame ideas, to make them feel fresh and original.

STRUGGLES WITH STRUCTURE: Funfear is a linear story – the plot works in a straight line, going from the beginning, to the end. Think of a story you might like to write – does that work in a linear way too? You might prefer to start at the middle, or even at the end. Funfear uses chapter headings too – wordtamers can really enjoy trying these out. But what about a story with no chapters? Or one told in Part One and Part Two? Maybe you could have two or more characters telling chunks of the story from their own point of view.

Look at your ideas, and think what might work best for your story.

MASTERING IMPACT: Short sentences create drama. They build tension. Long sentences give the reader a bit of room to breathe. Wordtamers know they need to use both, to make their writing as powerful as possible. Too many short sentences can feel stilted, but too many long sentences get confusing. Mixing them together will get the best results – but that's where the skill comes in. Good wordtamers know exactly when to use which sort. **Take a scene from your own idea, and try some training using long and short sentences.**

A POLISHED PERFORMANCE: Most wordtamers write drafts, experimenting with all the above possibilities before they start. Once they've chosen style and structure, and mastered 'impact', they can write their early drafts – but right at the end they still need to go back and give their story that final polish. Skilled wordtamers check for spelling mistakes, and punctuation problems. But they also go through check for special words, or for ways to make sentences feel special. Below are the first and last drafts of a sentence in Funfear.

Draft 1: The horse pranced round as the roundabout turned. It had yellow eyes and its hooves were painted gold.
Draft 2: The roundabout horse had magical yellow eyes. It plunged and rose, its golden hooves prancing.

Notice how the words are more vivid, but the meaning stays the same.

Take a sentence, or paragraph, from your own idea. Check the spelling and punctuation – but THEN look over it again, and see if you can think of descriptive words to make it even stronger.

AND FINALLY, SOME LAST, WELL TAMED WORDS FROM THE GUV'NOR

"I hope your training has got you trembling with anticipation, poised on the high wire of your imagination, spinning somersaults with words. But there's more – so much more …

… tame new creative ideas at the crazy funfair of possibilities:

www.wordtamer.co.uk

Meet me in my role as wordtamer, and meet Judy Waite in her role as author.

Between us we will help you sink your teeth into the wild and wonderful world of writing – unless, of course, the wild and wonderful world of writing sinks its teeth into you first!

HAPPY WRITING!

The Guv'nor

THE GRAND FINALE

FUNFEAR HAS BEEN TRAINED AND TAMED WITH THE HELP OF A STAR TEAM OF APPRENTICE TRAINERS.

Judy Waite would like to bring to the ring the following apprentice wordtamers, who showed such energy, spirit and raw courage in the face of so many wild words – when you hear your name, please step forward and take a bow:

LOCKS HEATH JUNIOR SCHOOL 2010 – 2011:

The sparkly bright editors – superstar readers who read and wrote reviews, and helped the early versions grow:

DAN, KEELEY, HENRY, ISOBEL, SIAN, LLOYD, AMY, EVIE, KATIE

And all the creative trainees who tamed and trained their own words at the 'after school' wordtamer funfairs:

EMILY B, HARRY, DYLAN, ANNABEL, JAMES, KIERON, ROSS, GRACE, EMILY M, KEELEY, SIMRAN, KATHERINE, RACHEL, PHILIPPA, EMILY B, MATTHEW, GEMMA, JADE, AMBER, NIAMH, HOLLY

And the Best Ever Grown-Up awards go to those star spangled assistants who helped keep the words clean, fed and regularly watered:

ANDY CLARKE

(Creative Writing Group: Word-Acrobatics Agility Expert)

SUE CLARKSON

(Creative Writing After School Club: Word-Charmer Extraordinaire)

And one extra dazzling glitter of thanks goes to:

KATE WILLIAMS:

Superstar Copy Editor with endless words of wisdom of her own!

Further author information, or to email questions, visit:

www.judywaite.com

Lightning Source UK Ltd.
Milton Keynes UK
UKOW050733311011

181216UK00001B/30/P